Praise for *Thugs and the Women Who Love Them*

"It's Gangsta and coming from a female point of view.
Can't wait for Part II."
—"The Ghost" Styles P

"People are trying to have sequels to their books after yours
came out. I smile because the original person has set the tone.
Keep writing!"
—Tru, Tru Books, Hartford, CT

"It's Gangsta, Gangsta! Love your work!"
—Project Pat, Three 6 Mafia

"*Thugs and the Women Who Love Them* reminds me of
another great black author, Donald Goines."
—Kenneth "Supreme" McGriff

"Wahida Clark . . . has a prefect sense of timing with her first
novel *Thugs and the Women Who Love Them*. A novel that takes a
look at reality and the rough friction of life. A guaranteed
'Hood Classic' . . . You won't be able to put it down."
—Freeze "Free Money," The Game

THUGS
and the Women
Who Love Them

WAHIDA CLARK

Chrissy,
Thanks for
the support
Wahida

Dafina
BOOKS

KENSINGTON PUBLISHING CORP.
http://www.kensingtonbooks.com

DAFINA BOOKS are published by

Kensington Publishing Corp.
850 Third Avenue
New York, NY 10022

All Kensington titles, imprints and distributed lines are available at special quantity discounts for bulk purchases for sales promotion, premiums, fund-raising, educational or institutional use.

Special book excerpts or customized printings can also be created to fit specific needs. For details, write or phone the office of the Kensington Special Sales Manager: Kensington Publishing Corp., 850 Third Avenue, New York, NY 10022. Attn. Special Sales Department. Phone: 1-800-221-2647.

Dafina Books and the Dafina logo Reg. U.S. Pat. & TM Off.

ISBN 0-7582-1286-0

First Kensington Trade Paperback Printing: December 2005
10 9 8 7

Printed in the United States of America

*This book is dedicated to all the brothas and sistahs on lockdown,
and to the entire Hip-Hop generation.
Thank you for making this, the first underground street novel,
to go triple platinum!*

Acknowledgments

All praise and thanks is forever due to the Creator, for without Him this would not be possible. I thank Him for placing all of the needed resources in my path.

To my soul mate, thanks for your vision, inspiration, and most important, your patience with me. Much love. To our daughters, Hasana and Muquarrabun, you two are such a blessing. D. Deering, thanks for your free advice on contracts and editing. Treena Wright, my friend thank you for feelin' this book as if it was your own.

First, to my typist and most dependable partna, Kisha; even though you whined, cried and complained 90 percent of the time and delivered a baby boy in the middle of this project, I got much love for you. I understand that not everyone is a workaholic like myself. To my other typists, Nobel, Hafida, and Samataha, thank you. Thank God for editors. I love what you did. Thank you.

To the first Atwood crew, those sistahs who were my first readers when it was on yellow notebook paper in my sloppy handwriting: Melissa Long and Lil' Memphis. To those sistahs who thought I should be writing instead of eating, sleeping, or breathing: Mecca, LoLo, and Shanna P.

To the rest of you who passed the yellow pages around and was just as excited as myself: Monica C., April C., Twigg, Miranda, Dana, Tammy, Cassie, Maggie, Daniele, Duresha, who also does my hair, Big Meeka, Neicey B., Tanya, K.K. Hatcher, Shawn K., Simone, Pauletta B., and Lucky. Thanks, K.K. Wall for sending a copy to Free of *106 and Park* and to the two sistahs who can read an entire novel in a few hours and whose opinion I highly respect; Ms. Belinda Marshal and Teesa Little. When they said this was good, I knew it was on! Thanks, Michelle D., for snapping my picture for this novel.

Thanks to *The Doug Banks* morning *Show* and Walt Baby Love for keeping me up in the morning while I was cranking out the pages. Thanks to Lexington's 107.9 *The Beat*. Thanks to Maxwell, Mary J. Blige, Toni Braxton, Marvin Gaye, Jaheim, Jadakiss, Case, Carl Thomas, and Ginuwine for making the music that helped me keep my flow.

Thanks to the C.O.s who made copies for me when the raggedy-ass inmate copy machine was broken (which was all of the time): Contreras, Martin, Henderson, D. Logan, S. Logan, Grier, Fox, Goins, Buttrey, Byrd, Doyle, Garrett, O'Brian, Breathett, and last but not least, K. Donovan.

Thanks to all the Black book clubs. Thanks to all the Black book-stores who put me on their bookshelves. Thanks to everyone I forgot to mention, and special thanks to all the Black authors who blazed the path before me. My biggest ups to Carl Weber, who wasted no time—and jumped immediately on this project. Thanks!

Special thanks to the authors who wrote me back: Teri Woods, Roy Glenn and especially Sonia Caulton, who told me to make sure that I write every day.

Thanks to my mom, dad, my lil' bro Mel, Aunt Ginger, Aunt Marva, Ann, and Carla. To my peeps, Shakira, Qurana, and Al-Nisa, who let me blow up their phone bills and never complained (not to me, at least). 'Preciate the love. Peace and one love to everyone I forgot to mention, and to all who wrote me, sent me money, books, and magazines.

If you'd like to holla at your girl, please write me at:

Wahida Clark
c/o Kisha Upshaw
P.O. Box 8520
Newark, NJ 07108

PART ONE

Angel

Chapter 1

"Thank you very much, Ms. Thompson, and please come again." The saleswoman smiled, shaking Angel's hand eagerly before she handed her three Wilson's Leather boutique shopping bags and a receipt.

"No, thank *you*," Angel replied. "And I'll be sure to tell all my friends about your store."

As she headed to the door, Angel turned to look at the woman, and she had to laugh. The salesgirl had picked up a calculator and was furiously punching in numbers, obviously calculating her commission on the $4,400.00 purchase Angel had just made. Too bad she had no idea that the check Angel had written was from a stolen checkbook, and the account had been closed for months. So Angel walked out of Wilson's with three big shopping bags filled with lots of items she would sell and a few for herself.

This was Angel's hustle to keep cash in her pockets. Going to law school was no easy task. It was a full-time job in itself. Trying to work *and* study just didn't work for her at all. There was no way she'd be able to finish school a semester early with a full-time job. She had to do one or the other, so she choose school.

She'd already managed to get her Bachelor's degree in three years. Now her goal was to graduate the same time as her home-girls: Roz, Kyra, and Jaz.

Angel did some window shopping on the way to her car. Oxford Valley Mall was the perfect place for Angel to run her game. The clerks were cordial and all the stores were very check friendly. She assumed the stores must have had some good insurance because she and every other hustler she knew had been wearing them out. Still, she knew her good luck couldn't last forever in this place. That's why she'd decided that after tonight she wouldn't be back. The last time she was at Oxford Valley she wrote almost $12,000.00 worth of bad checks. She planned on doing about the same tonight, if not more.

The merchandise she got from Wilson's would easily sell for between $1,800.00 and $2,200.00. Her fence, Rashid, usually bought all of the handbags and jewelry she could bring him. Way back, she and Rashid had been a couple, until Angel found out that she wasn't his only woman. Actually, she was one of three women who Rashid had scattered throughout the city. They'd only been involved for about six months, so it wasn't that tough for Angel to break things off. She still kept their business relationship open, though. After all, he was the best fence around, and she was looking forward to collecting from him after tonight.

Angel spotted a tennis bracelet in the window of Zales that she couldn't resist, but the Wilson's bags were starting to hurt her arms. So she decided to put the bags in her car and then come back for the bracelet. She had just squeezed onto the escalator that led to the first floor level when she noticed a woman staring at her from the up escalator. Angel did a double take as they passed each other. She realized the woman was a clerk who worked at one of the perfume counters at Macy's. Apparently, the woman remembered her, too.

A damn perfume clerk! Angel laughed to herself. Why couldn't it at least have been a jewelry store? Somewhere that she'd bilked for thousands of dollars instead of a couple of hundred. But when she looked up, Angel wasn't so amused anymore.

The tall, skinny clerk had stepped off the escalator at the second floor and was motioning to one of the mall's toy store cops. Angel was glad she had on some flat shoes. She stepped off the escalator and walked fast, in search of the nearest exit that would lead to her parked car. When she glanced back, she saw that the skinny clerk and a toy cop were on their way down the escalator. Angel got a firm grip on her bags and took off running.

"Excuse me! I need to catch my bus!" She was loud but polite as she swerved in and around the several crowds of people standing around the food court. "Sorry! Pardon me!" She apologized as she bumped a little boy in the head with her bags.

Angel ran right past the bus that was picking up the mall passengers. "Fuck!" She screamed as she realized that her car was parked way around the other side of the mall. She felt like crying, but she kept running. Her fingers and arms were burning from the heavy bags she was carrying. A red van provided a place for her to hide behind, to catch her breath and see where the toy cop was. She went to the edge of the van and peeked around. A meddling shopper was standing next to a toy cop—she was pointing in her direction. *Goddamn Good Samaritan!* Angel ducked down and was moving between the parked cars as fast as she could. She had broken into a sweat.

"Shit!" She yelled as she set off a car alarm on a silver BMW. She stood up so she could run even faster. Behind her, the toy cop was fumbling with his radio, trying to talk into it and chase her at the same time. She was glad that he was fat, because he wasn't moving very fast.

"Where's my fuckin' car?" She was trying not to panic. Her fingers and arms were now in super burn mode. The thought that she left the driver's side open for reasons like this one soothed her a little bit. A spare ignition key was stuffed in her bra.

I'd be a'ight if I could just find my damn car now! She thought.

Toy cop was trying to gain on her.

"Yes! Yes! Thank you, Lord!" She spotted her green Honda Civic. "Fuck!" She breathed out fire when she saw orange dice hanging from the rearview mirror. "That's not my car!" She ran faster.

"Come here! I just want to . . . talk to you!" Toy cop barely got out those words.

Angel ran faster. She spotted another green Honda four cars over. "Please forgive me, Lord, for cussing. Please let this be my car!" This time she looked at the license plate. "Oh, fuck!" She had stolen tags. She noticed the strawberry air freshener hanging down and smiled. "That's my car."

She didn't even remember opening the door and stuffing the bags onto the passenger seat. She only knew that she had to start the car. She put the car in reverse. When she backed up, she hit a station wagon. Another Good Samaritan was performing their "civic duty" by blocking her in. Angel rolled the window down and screamed.

"Move the fuck outta my way or I'm gonna knock your doors in!" She rolled her car window back up just as toy top grabbed the door handle and tried to open the door. Luckily it was locked. He started banging on the window and calling for help on his radio. Angel ignored him. She backed up again into the station wagon. This time the Good Samaritan was cursing as he moved the station wagon out of Angel's way. Toy cop was banging on the hood, commanding Angel to stop as she finally backed out of her parking space and floored it. She headed to the nearest exit, prayed, and thanked God for helping her out of that close call. If she got busted, then her man Keenan would know what she'd been up to—not to mention her mom. She couldn't afford for that to happen.

Chapter 2

"I'm not one of your fucking hos," Angel screamed as she threw the iron at Snake. He was almost out the door when the iron hit him on the back of the neck. He turned to go after Angel, but she slammed the bedroom door and locked it.

"Get the fuck out of my house," she yelled.

"I hate you!"

Snake tried to break the doorknob, but he jammed it instead. He started banging on the door, trying to break it down.

"Get the fuck out my house," Angel screamed again.

"I pay the rent here!" Snake yelled.

"I don't give a fuck!"

Snake turned around, did a karate kick, and his leg went smashing through the door. He reached inside, turned the knob, and it fell to the floor. Angel was rummaging through the closet trying to find a bat, a stick, an axe, anything. She was not going to let Snake beat her down without giving him a fight. She wasn't going out like that. She barely managed to pick up a metal hanger and straighten out the hook when he grabbed her by her hair. She swung around and sliced him across the cheek with her fresh-made weapon.

"Awwh, fuck!" He gasped as the blood squirted out.

He banged her head against the radiator. Angel gritted her teeth as a few trickles of blood wet her forehead. Snake really didn't want to hurt her, so he just pushed her face into the floor. She screamed for her mother. Angel's mom, Julia, didn't even move from the desk where she was sitting. She just yelled for Snake to leave and then mumbled about how tired she was of both of them. After all, what could she say that would make a damn bit of difference? Snake and Angel had been messing around for almost two years. Plus, he paid the rent, Angel's tuition, and whatever else Julia needed. All she had to do was ask, and he paid. She was used to their violent relationship. Just as long as he didn't turn her daughter out, 'cause then she would have to kill him.

Snake calmed down a little when he heard her mother's voice. He inspected the bloodstains on his dark, olive-colored Versace shirt with the snakeskin buttons, and smacked Angel one more time. Angel, still propped on the floor, kicked him in the stomach and called him a punk bitch as she reached for her 9mm. She held it with both hands and aimed at his face. Snake just stood there and looked at those sexy hazel eyes, perky nose, and smooth, sensual lips, which were now in a pout.

"Put down the gun, baby."

She didn't move an inch. Blood was slowly dripping down her forehead. It really turned Snake on when she was pissed at him and fought back. Maybe that's why his attraction to her was so strong. She was definitely a challenge to him, and he liked a challenge. He had no respect for females who didn't fight back.

Angel was still lying there with the 9mm cocked, pointing it at him. She was drenched in sweat and her nipples were protruding through the tight, see-through blouse she had on. Eyeing those luscious nipples of hers made Snake's dick hard. He loved sucking on those sweet, round nipples. Since Snake's thinking went from his head down to his dick, now he had to figure out how he could get some. He figured she wouldn't give him any if she was too pissed. Little did Snake know that when Angel's eyes shot down and saw Snake's hard dick, it would be much easier than he thought.

Damn, Angel said to herself. *I don't wanna give in to him now. Not this easy.* As she lay there looking up at 6-foot-3 Snake, her eyes roamed his cold, piercing eyes, jet-black, wavy hair and muscular arms. All she could focus on was how fine he was and how he could make her come for what seemed like forever. She could see why once his whores got a taste of that dick they would go nowhere. It didn't matter that he put his foot up their asses every chance he got. They were there for the long haul.

Angel got up off the floor and asked Snake in a squeaky voice to please leave. She decided to hide her "9" in a new spot, this time on the top shelf in her closet. As she raised up, Snake noticed the long rip in her skirt that exposed her smooth, yellow thighs. Snake's dick was still hard as he reached for his silk handkerchief and started wiping the blood off the side of his face. He didn't say anything, nor did he move from the spot where he was standing.

They both looked around in amazement at the mess they'd just made. The iron was shattered to pieces, the ironing board was upside down, there was a huge hole in the bedroom door, and pillows and blankets lay on the floor. On top of that, Angel's Chanel skirt was ripped and she had a huge, ugly knot on her forehead.

"Come here, baby," Snake said. "I'm sorry."

Angel was already standing in front of the dresser, looking

herself over in the mirror. Her hair was all over the place. The knot on her forehead spattered small drops of blood on her blouse.

Snake eased over to where she stood.

"Baby, you are so fuckin' hot when you get angry."

"What kind of lame compliment is that?" Angel sucked her teeth. "You being a so-called pimp daddy, I know you can come better than that." *This nigga makes me sick*, she thought to herself. "Look, nigga, I'm gonna say this only once. Are you listening?"

"I'm listening."

"This is the last fucking time we have a fight. Trust and believe, if you ever hit me again, I'm gonna blow your fucking brains out. Look at this fuckin' knot on my head." She examined it again in the mirror. "The last time. Do you understand me?"

"I hear you."

"I know you hear me. But do you understand? Tell me you fuckin' understand!" she yelled.

"I understand, baby. Damn!"

Snake inched up closer to her, resting his hard dick on her soft behind. Angel didn't protest. It felt good, but she was trying not to let Snake know it.

"Look, baby, all I'm saying is that you always look good to me. When you wake up in the morning, if you got a big knot on your forehead, it don't matter. You could be wearing rags!"

Snake reached up and started playing with her nipples. They both watched in the mirror as her nipples got harder. Angel's cheeks were turning redder.

"I'm sorry, baby. I didn't mean to lose my temper like that," he whispered in her ear.

"I'm not one of your whores, Keenan." She refused to call him by his nickname.

"I know, baby. You know I love you, and I never mean to hurt you," Snake whispered in her ear.

"Then why in the hell did you come in here hitting me like that?"

"Because, baby, I told you I didn't want you around that nigga Dwayne. He ain't shit! Study group or no fuckin' study group."

"I told you we have two classes together. He's a square, and there is no attraction there. You are my man. Why can't you just let it go? How could you be so fucking insecure?"

"I know, baby, but you're spending just a little too much time with him and I already told you I don't like it. I'm a pimp, baby. I know who's a square and who ain't."

"You don't own me, Keenan. I have to handle my business."

Snake's hands were already sliding up under Angel's skirt and he was sliding her panties down. He slipped two fingers up her pussy and licked her neck. Her pussy quickly became drenched with her love juices. *I knew she was turned on,* Snake thought to himself. *I don't know why she likes to play hard.*

Angel, mumbling through her moans, told Snake to postpone this and come over later, because her mom and little sister were in the next room. Snake, ignoring her, pushed her over and unzipped his Versace pants. They fell to the floor. He put on a condom and then rammed his rod into her pussy in one quick motion. Angel shrieked in pleasure.

"Damn, baby, that feels sooooo good," she moaned as the hot juices flowed down her thighs. Snake stroked and stroked until Angel's body started twitching, then went limp. She sprawled out over the dresser. Snake, still deep inside her, leaned over and kissed her neck roughly.

"I'll catch up with you later." He pulled out and pulled off the condom, fixed his clothes and walked out of the bedroom. Angel was still sprawled across the dresser trying to catch her breath.

Julia was still posted at her desk doing paperwork, while Angel's twelve-year-old sister, Carmen, had her head stuck in the refrigerator. Neither one of them said anything to Snake as he walked out the front door.

Chapter 3

Snake closed the apartment door and headed down the hall-way toward the elevator. As he pushed the down button, his cell phone vibrated. He flipped open the phone.

"I have a Nell calling collect. Will you accept the charges?" It was the dry voice of an operator.

"Yeah," said Snake.

"What's up?" Snake asked irritably.

"I've been calling you all day. Where the hell you been and why haven't you been answering the phone? I could've been dying!" Big Nell complained.

"Don't ask me questions. I run this shit!" Snake yelled into the phone.

Big Nell was Snake's oldest whore. She had been on the stroll for Snake for almost six years now, and she lived up to her name. She had big eyes, a big mouth, big legs, big tits, and a big, big ass. The white johns were in love with her, but Snake was notic-ing that her mouth was getting feistier than usual. It was proba-bly because he'd been too busy to put his size eleven snakeskin shoes up her wide ass. He was going to do that as soon as he saw her.

"I got busted last night at the Radisson. It's seventeen hundred to bail me out."

"You was lying on your back for seven hours and you don't have seventeen hundred? You think I'm crazy?"

"Snake, baby, the police took all my money, and I even had to suck two of their dicks. I'll get everything back for you."

Snake hung up on her. The elevator still didn't come.

"Damn thing must be broke," he muttered. "I wish she would move out this building."

Snake headed for the stairs. At the bottom of the first flight he noticed one of his whores. Lexus was six feet tall with a beautiful body, but her greatest asset was those pretty, long curvaceous legs. She looked like Tyra Banks. She was sitting at the top of the stairwell in the corner in a deep nod, her beige, silk, T-strap Chanel dress clinging tightly to her curves. Her thighs were exposed and her long legs stretched to the third step. Her hair hung wildly and saliva spilled out of the corner of her mouth. Lexus was totally oblivious to everything around her, including mean-ass Snake hovering over her.

I know this bitch ain't high, Snake thought to himself. He grabbed her arm to examine it and to confirm the needle holes scarring her pretty, brown complexion. She didn't even feel Snake holding her arm up.

"You dumb bitch!" he yelled as he kicked her on the thigh.

Lexus jumped up and slurred, "Hey, Daddy, I feel so sick. I was just sitting here resting and waiting for you." She rubbed her thigh where Snake had just kicked her.

He slapped her in the face.

"You lying bitch! How are you waitin' on me and you didn't even know I was here?"

Snake grabbed her little Fendi bag and emptied the contents on the stairwell floor. A bottle of Obsession, a half pack of

Newports, condoms, one hundred and eighty dollars, two bags of dope and the works to go with it, fell onto the steps.

Lexus's eyes grew wide in terror as Snake examined the purse contents. Lexus knew what was coming.

"Give me the rest of my damn money!" Snake's words sliced through Lexus's stomach.

Her trembling hands slid between her legs and pulled out a plastic bag. She handed the money to Snake and tried to apologize her way out of an ass whipping. As he counted the money, fear was beginning to make her high wear off. He put the three hundred and forty dollars into his wallet. Lexus's knees got weak as she felt his cold eyes staring at her.

"Lexus." He stared into her eyes. "You know the fuckin' policy. No drugs! Daddy ain't wastin' his fuckin' money on dope. That's money that goes on this fuckin' Chanel dress you got on." He slapped her. "That's money that goes for the nice fuckin' roof I keep over your head!"

He grabbed her around her neck and tried his best to choke her to death. When Snake got mad at his whores he lost all of his common sense. Instead of thinking logically that these women were his bread and butter, he would try his best to kill them. He had succeeded with four of them in the past.

Lexus was kicking and trying to pull Snake's tight grip from around her neck. Her complexion was no longer chocolate coffee. It was now blue. With one quick motion, he slung her down the flight of stairs. Her body slammed against the stairwell door. Snake walked down the flight of stairs and picked her up. He started to punch her in the face. As she weakly tried to cover herself from the brutal blows, he dropped her to the floor and started kicking her. The kicks turned to stomps. Lexus could no longer breathe. Her entire body felt numb.

"Please," she begged. "Please stop it, Daddy!" She cried. "I swear that was my last fix," she cried out.

Snake was startled that she had that much energy left to talk. He stood still and just stared at her, breathing heavy.

"Get your dope fiend ass up. Go somewhere and clean up." He straightened out his clothes and went toward the front exit. *Pimpin' ain't easy*, he thought to himself.

When he walked out into the fresh air he almost tripped over Angel's homegirls. Here stood Roz, Jaz, and Kyra, who was Angel's first cousin.

"This ain't my fucking day," he said.

"Seeing you don't make it our fucking day either," Kyra replied.

He disliked the threesome, and he knew the feelings were mutual. There was especially bad blood between him and Kyra. Angel always took Kyra's side over Snake's when there was a problem, and that drove him crazy. But he still had to give them their props. At least they were trying to do something with their lives. They were determined not to let the ghetto take them out.

Kyra noticed the fresh slash across Snake's cheek and the blood on his shirt.

"You prick! If she's hurt I'm gonna kill you myself, you fake-ass pimp," she yelled. "I hate you! I don't know why her crazy ass won't leave you alone."

"Fuck him!" yelled Roz. "If she's hurt, we're coming after you." She pointed at Snake.

"All of you bitches can go to hell. That's my woman. I'm fucking her, not y'all," he said with a sarcastic grin.

That's just why I don't like them. They got too much mouth, he thought to himself as he turned and walked to his Benz.

"You're gonna get yours. You watch!" Jaz yelled. When the

trio reached the apartment and rang the buzzer, Angel's little sister Carmen answered the door. They pushed her aside and ran straight to Angel's bedroom. When they saw the hole in the door they started screaming Angel's name. She was already in the bathroom cleaning herself up. The crew looked around the room. It was still in shambles. The closet door was wide open, showing the open shoe boxes, shoes, and clothes all over the floor. Jaz ran to the bathroom door and started banging on it.

Angel came out of the bathroom all cleaned up, looking fine except for the knot on her forehead. Her long tresses were pulled back into a ponytail. She wore some form-fitting Filth Mart jeans and a white Prada belly blouse.

Jaz, who was the most perceptive of the crew, looked at the glow on Angel's face and assessed the situation.

"After he whipped your ass you fucked him, didn't you?" She sucked her teeth and rolled her eyes, not giving Angel a chance to answer. "What is the matter with you? One of these days he's gonna kill you. What do you see in that fuckin' pimp?" She was furious.

"I can't help it." Angel burst out crying. All three girls rushed over to Angel and surrounded her in a group hug.

"Damn you, Angel," Kyra said.

"I can't help it. It's just that this is the kind of relationship we have. You wouldn't understand. We've been together for almost two years, and I love him. I'm crazy about him. He's responsible, and he helps us out a whole lot. If it wasn't for him my college tuition wouldn't be paid. And when my mom got sick we would have been in the streets. Plus,"—she gave them a sly smile—"I whip his ass. Y'all know he got the bruises to show it."

They all burst out laughing.

"I ain't scared of that ma'fucka." Angel was trying to sound like Bernie Mac. "I laid down the law tonight and told him no more fighting or else I'ma blow his fuckin' brains out."

"Well, your hot ass is gonna end up dead, and I ain't going to the funeral," Kyra said. "I am sick and tired of both of you."

"Please, can y'all help me clean up this mess?" Angel pleaded.

Chapter 4

Angel was born Angel Denise Smith, second oldest of four children. When she was born, her mother looked at her high yellow skin, hazel eyes, and silky dark brown hair and immediately knew she should be called Angel. As she grew, everyone always remarked that she was the spitting image of her mother. She was tall and slender at 5 feet 10 inches, and for some reason, until the 7th grade she still had all her baby teeth. The girls would call her stuck up, or Miss Prissy, when she was growing up. And they were right—Angel was beautiful and she knew it.

Her mother, Julia Smith, had been an insurance agent for the last eight years, but before that she worked in the hospital cafeteria as head cook. Angel's father was a foreman at one of the biggest auto paint shops in the city. Everyone called him Big Red because he was 6 feet 5 inches and high yellow, with dark red hair. Between Big Red and Julia both holding down steady employment, Angel and her siblings were raised with a little more comfort than most of the other kids growing up in the hood.

Angel loved and looked up to her eldest brother, Willie Right. He earned the nickname Willie Right because he always insisted he was right, even when he knew he was wrong.

When Angel was only nine years old and he was fourteen, she remembered how Willie Right was bragging to everyone. His daddy, Big Red, was going to get him a moped dirt bike for Christmas. He went so far as to carry the picture of the black and red motorbike in his back pocket to flash to anyone who was interested. He told nine-year-old Angel, and Mark, who was eight, that he was not going to give them a ride on it because they were too little. This was a big kid's bike.

He bragged about the dirt bike for months. He even brought home straight A's on his report card the semester before Christmas just to make sure. He wanted to hear no excuses when it was time for Big Red to deliver.

All of Willie's friends looked up to him. He had both of his parents living at home, his clothes were nicer than the rest of the crew's, and he was very smart. Plus, Willie Right always scored with the hottest girls. He would leave out no details when telling his partners about his scores. Willie Right was living large in their eyes, plus, they couldn't wait to ride around on the dirt bike with Willie, in front of all the honeys.

As Christmas neared, Big Red started to give more thought to the idea of his eldest son riding on a motor dirt bike. He discussed it with Julia. The more he thought about it, the more he disliked the idea. It was dangerous, and too many of the kids were getting jacked for their expensive things. He had enough problems keeping Willie off the drugs and out of trouble. He was not about to lose his son over a bike. So Big Red decided to buy all three of his kids Schwinn ten-speed bicycles. Of course, Angel and Mark were ecstatic, but Willie was pissed off. He had his heart set on that black and red dirt bike. Plus, he had his boys and the honeys to impress. Dangerous didn't matter to Willie Right.

When Willie's homeboys found out that Willie got a bicycle

instead of the motorbike, they clowned him something awful. So Willie, furious and embarrassed as hell, made him a pipe bomb, went down to the auto paint shop where Big Red worked, and torched the joint. Willie was smart, but dumb enough to torch the joint in broad daylight. Even though the shop was closed, the few eyewitnesses in the area knew he was Big Red's son. And everybody knew Big Red. Just about everything in the shop was flammable, so it didn't take but a couple of minutes for a loud explosion and flames to reach the sky. The flames were so high the whole west side of town could see the smoke.

Willie had made it safely home where he was posted on his front porch. He grinned as he watched the black smoke circle the clouds. His boys, Donny, Plug, Mo, and Justice sat down on his stairs and watched the smoke, listening to Willie Right, who knew he was wrong, describe how he made the pipe bomb and burned the shop down to the ground. They had been sitting there for almost an hour.

"My dad loves that shop more than he loves me. Now who's he going to love more?" Willie declared.

Just as Willie got those words out of his mouth, nine police cars came flying down the street. All of his homeboys scattered like roaches running from a can of Raid. Willie ran into the house to get Big Red's shotgun.

When Julia saw what her fourteen-year-old son was doing, she ran toward him and tried her best to take the gun from him.

"I ain't going out like that!" He kept screaming.

Angel and Mark stood watching as Willie pushed their mom down and bolted for the door.

"Get upstairs! Now!" Julia screamed at Angel and Mark.

Angel and Mark didn't move. They gazed out the window in horror at all the police cars, then at their big brother, holding their daddy's big gun.

23

"Put down the gun and put your hands up in the air!" screamed the officer through the bullhorn.

"You put your gun down and put your hands up in the air!" yelled Willie.

"I repeat, and this is my last time . . ."

The sentence was interrupted when Willie cocked the shotgun and pointed it at the officer on the bullhorn.

"Put the gun down, Willie," sobbed Julia.

"I repeat, put down your fucking gun and put your hands over your head!" yelled the police officer.

Willie Right refused to put the gun down, and the trigger-happy police went to firing at Willie right there on the front porch. His body moved, jerked and fell as if he were in a movie and the scene was playing in slow motion. They shot him so many times that Willie's tall, thin body was ripped and torn to pieces. Angel, Mark, and Julia watched the whole horrifying scene from the window. Now, Willie Right's body pieces lay shredded up on their front porch.

They didn't even know that Big Red was outside in handcuffs, sitting in the back of one of the police cars. He had punched one of the police officers, and was even prepared to take the rap for his son. Instead, he watched helplessly as his son's life was taken over a dirt bike that he refused to buy.

Big Red was so distraught about the loss of his son that he left his family, never to be seen or heard from again. He didn't even know that he left Julia pregnant. She was left alone to raise Angel, Mark, and the soon-to-be-born Carmen.

Julia refused to go on welfare. She tried to make ends meet on her salary from the hospital cafeteria, but things were tough. Raising three kids was getting more and more expensive. She eventually lost the house that she and Big Red struggled so hard to keep, and had to move her family into the Roger Gardens projects.

After years of struggling, one of Big Red's friends finally helped her get a job as a clerk at an insurance company. Julia decided to go to school at night to get her license and become a full-fledged insurance agent. They were struggling, but Julia was determined her kids would have a chance to move out of the projects. She pursued her career, and she made sure the kids went to school, did their homework and made the honor roll. Julia was determined that they would make something of themselves in spite of the tragedy they had faced.

Chapter 5

That was ten years ago. Julia and her three kids moved out of the projects into a 15-story apartment building on the west side of town. Times were not as hard because of Angel's man, Snake. And Julia's dream of her children succeeding was becoming a reality. Angel was working toward her law degree and Mark was working on his Associates degree in broadcasting. Carmen, following her siblings' example, was an honor roll student. Julia let herself believe they had really accomplished something. As much as possible, she just ignored the fact that her daughter was dating a pimp.

When Angel first introduced her to Snake, Julia had practically fainted. She knew him as Lil' Keenan when he was just a kid, and she also knew that he came from a long line of pimps. His daddy was a pimp before he got stabbed to death. Snake also had four pimp uncles.

She had slapped Angel over and over, screaming at her, wanting to know how a college girl could turn into a ho. Why couldn't she stay away from that pimp? Angel moved out of the house, in with Kyra, and didn't speak to her mom for several months. Julia kept calling Kyra's mom to secretly check up on her daughter.

Angel was still going to college, working, and of course, laying up with Snake, the pimp. When she couldn't stand it anymore, Julia finally broke down and asked her daughter to come back home. Of course, Angel was glad to move back in. She missed her mom, brother, and her sister.

Julia was pleasantly surprised when Angel showed up back home. She had really underestimated her daughter's strength. Angel was a confident and strong-willed person, who wasn't about to be turned out by Snake, and he knew that. She could think for herself. That's what Snake liked about her. She was someone who could balance him out. Someone to settle down with. After all the whores he'd dealt with, Snake respected a woman who wouldn't let him beat her down physically or mentally.

As Snake put his foot on the brake of his Mercedes 500, he reminisced back to the day when he'd first laid eyes on those long, smooth, yellow legs. Those were the first things that caught Snake's eyes. He considered himself a connoisseur of legs. His eyes roamed from those long, curvaceous beauties to that perfectly round ass to those perky, young tits. He was floored. She wore a white, sleeveless, leather-front top with deep cleavage and a tight, cream-colored, pleated skirt. Snake grabbed his dick and put it along his thigh because it had gotten hard.

Angel could feel the heat of a dog's roaming eyes all over her body. She knew that she was a dog magnet. She had had her share of dogs, so at this point in time she was being extra careful and not giving in too soon. As Angel turned slyly around to see where the dog was, her books slipped to the floor.

Damn! she thought. *That's what I get for even thinking about giving a dog a bone.*

As she bent down to pick up her books, she noticed the black, snakeskin Versace shoes quickly coming her way. She smelled the Armani cologne. Snake didn't say a word; he just bent down, picked up the remaining books and handed them to her. *This bitch is fuckin' fine!* he almost said out loud.

"Thank you," she said.

"Oh, miss, that will be four dollars and eighty-seven cents," the cashier announced.

"Just a minute," Angel snapped.

Snake pulled out his wallet to pay for her meal. Angel's eyes were glued to the iced-up Rolex on Snake's wrist as he reached over and handed the cashier a 10-dollar bill. Before she even took her eyes off the Rolex, Snake had already turned and walked away. He was a pimp. He knew how to set his traps. The cashier yelled after him to get his change, but he just kept walking, slow, smooth, and with confidence.

As Angel eyed him from the back, she had to admit that she liked what she saw. He looked to be about 6 foot 3. He had dark, wavy hair and sideburns that were neatly cut. His stride was full of confidence and power. And watching it was all the more fun because he had the kind of butt that a woman loved to squeeze.

The tailor-made Armani suit, silk shirt, snakeskin shoes, iced-up Rolex and Armani cologne announced that *ole boy got it goin' on*, but Angel knew from hard-knock experience that you can't judge a thug by his cover. She had to check things out thoroughly. She grabbed her container of teriyaki steak and rice and quickly headed for the exit. When she got outside, she looked right and didn't see him. She turned left and still he was nowhere in sight. She sighed and put her hand on her hip. Snake was sitting in his Benz watching her every move. He knew that she would come looking for him.

"Works every time," he said.

Snake beeped that smooth Mercedes horn and rolled down

the passenger window. Angel checked out the "500" with the chrome rims. *This nigga thinks he's smooth*, she thought. She went over and peeked into the car. His Armani cologne smacked her in the face. She dropped a 10-dollar bill on the passenger seat.

"I can pay for my own meals. But thanks anyway." She quickly glanced at the manicured hand resting on the steering wheel.

Snake looked at her beautiful, pouted lips and said, "No problem. I assume you're one of them independent women."

"You damned right." She turned to walk away.

"So it's like that?"

Angel acted like she didn't hear him and kept on walking. Now it was her turn to set a trap. As she headed to her Honda Civic, she knew he wouldn't be far behind. She fumbled for her keys, opened the door, set her books on the backseat and the container of teriyaki steak and rice on the front seat. Once she turned the key in the ignition, the shiny black 500 pulled up in front of her, just as she'd expected. Snake got out of his car and walked toward her.

"What are you, stalking me now?"

"No. Just give me your phone number and I'm out."

Angel looked him up and down. *Damn! This nigga is fine*, she thought as she tried to suppress a smile.

"I don't give my number away to strangers."

"I'm not a stranger. I picked up your books from the floor, I tried to pay for your meal and I made sure you got to your car safely. Strangers don't do that."

Angel looked into his eyes. They were dark and cold, but everything else about him said he was all that. Angel liked the whole package.

"Give me your number." She tried to flip the script.

"I don't give my number to strangers," Snake answered, looking into her eyes.

"Oh, well. We're just deadlocked, then, aren't we?" She didn't look away from his stare.

"Deadlocked, huh? So, you must be a law student."

"Maybe, maybe not."

He had already seen the Rutgers parking sticker on her windshield.

"So, what's your name?"

"So, what's yours?" she teased.

Needless to say, Snake was enjoying this little game. "My friends call me Snake, but it's Keenan Hightower."

"My friends call me Angel, and it's Angel Smith. Now, may I go?"

"After I get your number."

"I'm listed," she snapped as she rolled up the window.

Snake smiled and turned back toward his car. He slid into his Benz, pushed number four on the CD player and pumped "Ascension" by Maxwell. Angel sat and watched the Benz ease around the corner.

"I think that went quite well," she spoke out loud to herself. "If he's all that, he'll find me."

Chapter 6

Little did she know that Snake was already on it. He picked up his cellular phone and dialed his boy, who ran the Black Studies Department at Rutgers.

"Rutgers University. How may I direct your call?"

"Buck Davis, please."

Snake leaned back in the driver's seat. While he waited, on hold, he cruised the hood to see what his whores were doing. He spotted Jade, his Asian ho. He swerved around the corner and beeped the horn. Jade spotted her daddy's car and ran toward it.

"Hey, Daddy!" she said in her Asian accent. "Here's $320.00."

She handed Snake the balled up cash and leaned in to kiss him on the cheek. When Jade puckered her lips, he hit her in the mouth with his cell phone. He bashed her once, and then again. The blood gushed from her mouth. She let out a groan. Tears welled up in her eyes. She knew not to say a word, because Snake was treacherous. Her trembling fingers reached into her purse and pulled out a handkerchief.

Snake screamed, "Bitch! What the fuck am I supposed to do with $320.00?" He threw the money back at her.

No, this nigga didn't, she thought to herself. When she bent down to pick it up, he opened the door and banged her in the head, knocking her to the ground. He glanced at the cell phone and saw that he had disconnected himself from Rutgers. This made him even madder.

"Get your little ass back out there!" he yelled as he sped off. "Damn bitches!"

As he stopped for a red light, the phone rang. Snake hit the answer button.

"What up, dawg!" It was Buck.

"How'd you know I called you?"

"I got fucking ESP, man. What you want?"

Buck and Snake had grown up together. They had been friends for almost twenty years, and though they had chosen separate paths, they always looked out for each other.

"I need a favor," Snake said. "I need you to get me a number."

"Don't you be recruiting our good, old-fashioned college girls for your stable," Buck joked.

"Man, I ain't recruiting nobody. This is some other business."

"Yeah, right. Then why you ain't got the number?" They both started laughing.

"Look, man, her name is Angel Smith."

"We got a lot of Smiths. Do you know how common that name is?"

"C'mon, man. You only got one Angel Smith who is a law student and drives a Honda Civic. I need a phone number and address."

"All right, calm down. I'll see what I can do." Buck hung up the phone.

Snake pulled over when he got to the Quality Inn. This was one of the joints where his whores were always working. The establishment gave Snake and his crew no problems. He parked the car and went into the lobby.

"Good evening, Mr. Hightower," the clerk greeted him.

Snake ignored him and headed for the double doors that led to the bar. Before he opened the glass doors, he stood and watched his hardest-working ho, Big Nell, talking to a john. While she talked and laughed with the john she was going through all of his pockets. The drunk fool didn't even notice. Snake watched as she lifted a big wad of cash from the pocket inside his jacket. Impressed by Nell's work, Snake opened the door and went to the back table, near the bathrooms.

Big Nell looked to be about thirty-two years old, but was only twenty-six. She was dark as a Hershey bar, looked Cuban, and the white johns loved every inch of her. She was their chocolate fantasy.

When Big Nell spotted Snake in the back she told the john she'd get back with him later. The john was feeling all over Big Nell's tits and ass.

"I'll catch you later, baby," she said as she squeezed his little prick.

"I can't wait, my chocolate sunflower," said the little white man. "I'll give you an extra fifty dollars if you do me right now."

Big Nell looked over at Snake sitting in the corner. She couldn't tell what mood he was in. She grabbed the man by the hand and pulled him toward the back corner, opposite Snake. The white john could hardly contain himself. He hurriedly pulled down his pants and briefs in one quick movement. His little pecker was already hard, and he was breathing even harder. Nell got down on her knees, put a rubber on him and sucked it for less than a minute before it went limp. When she stood up, she had his wallet in her hand. She gave it to him and he handed her $150.00.

"I'll catch you next time, my big white stallion," she said to the satisfied customer. She left him standing there with his butt showing.

"Hey, Daddy." She grinned as she slid next to Snake in the booth. "I've been trying to call you all afternoon."

As she was talking, she was pulling money rolls out of her panties, her bra, and her purse.

Snake counted the rolls of money. It came out to $1,100.00.

"I know you got more than this."

"That's it for now, Daddy. I'll have more later on."

Snake punched her in the face.

"Get the fuck up!" He grabbed her by the hair.

"I'ma get more, Daddy," she pleaded. "I swear."

Snake dragged her into the bathroom. He thought she must've kept the roll of money that he saw her lift from that john. But she didn't. Big Nell had given him every dollar she had on her. Snake started banging her head against the toilet. Big Nell was trying to loosen his grip off her hair. That was hurting more than the head banging. She started digging her nails into his hands. "Bitch, you must be crazy!" He let her hair go and started to kick her. His foot was landing blows against her stomach, her tits, her head and face. When she stopped screaming, he stopped kicking her. As Big Nell lay on the floor crying, he washed his hands, fixed his clothes and left the bathroom.

As he walked past the patrons, one drunk dude yelled, "Handle your business, gorilla pimp!" Snake left the lobby as quietly and smoothly as he came in. He jumped into his Benz and pulled off.

Chapter 7

As Snake got comfortable in the leather seat of his Benz, he felt like he needed a drink. He decided to relax himself by reminiscing about his early days with Angel. Thoughts of Angel always put him at ease.

After he got her number and address from his boy Buck, he started closing in. In his opinion, all women were bitches and whores, made to pimp. Angel, though, appeared to be a little different. He had to check himself for thinking like that, because he knew he couldn't get soft. You can't play the game and win, being soft. Still, he knew he had to have this woman.

Once he had her address, Snake had sent Angel a dozen red roses and a box of Godiva chocolates. On the card he had written, "You knew I would find you. Will pick you up at 8:00." Angel had told him about what happened when she got the roses and chocolates, and the story still made him smile. She'd kept asking the delivery guy, "Are you sure you have the right Angel Smith?" After he convinced her, "Yes, ma'am. I'm sure," she couldn't stop blushing. She breathed deeply to inhale the scent of the fresh roses. *This nigga thinks he is real smooth*, she thought. As she stood there daydreaming and smelling the roses, she forgot her three homegirls were in the room.

Smack! Smack! Roz clapped her hands.

"Earth to Angel! Earth to Angel!" Her friends laughed.

Angel turned around and smiled at her homies. Kyra jumped up and snatched the card out of Angel's hand and Jaz grabbed the chocolates. Angel's nose was still buried in the roses.

"You knew I would find you," said Kyra in her best imitation of a man's voice.

"What's the dilio, ho?" asked Jaz.

Angel kept grinning as she looked around the living room at the girls. They had already opened her box of chocolates and ate half the box.

"Y'all are so greedy!"

"Sorry. I'm PMS-ing." Kyra groaned.

"Forget that. What's his name, where does he work, and what kind of whip he got?" asked Roz in one breath.

"Why didn't you tell us about this one?" Jaz asked.

"You tryin' to keep him all for yourself?" asked Roz.

They all laughed. Angel told them about how she met Snake at the Steak Pub a few days ago. She told them how he picked up her books, paid for her meal, the Armani suit, the snakeskin shoes, and the Armani cologne. She saved the Rolex, Benz, and how he blocked her in the parking lot for last.

"Daaang!" said Kyra.

"What does he do?" asked Jaz.

"I'm not sure," Angel answered.

"What do he want with your skinny ass?" Roz asked.

"Shut up and don't be hatin' on a sister!" Angel joked.

"Well, we're just gonna have to wait here until he comes," Jaz and Roz said at the same time.

"I don't think so," said Angel. "I am escorting y'all to the door right now."

Angel started waving both arms toward the door. They all got the hint and stood up reluctantly, grumbling. Angel tried not to laugh at them. As they walked toward the front door, the girls said 'bye to Ms. Smith and hugged Angel.

"Have a good time. And be careful," Kyra said.

"I will. Love y'all." Angel blew them a kiss and closed the front door.

She headed toward her bedroom to get ready for a shower. It was almost 6:45. She turned on the hot water to steam up the bathroom. She wiped the steam off the bathroom mirror and started plucking her eyebrows, pondering what to wear. Her thoughts were running wild about how this evening would go. As she stepped into the hot, steamy shower she imagined him asking for some. If he did, she would try her best to decline, even though she was horny as hell. She had kept her legs closed for almost seven and a half months. Before she turned off the hot steam, she put moisturizer all over her body. She turned off the water, grabbed her towel and headed into her bedroom.

When she opened the door, her sister Carmen and her best friend Lakiyah were sitting on her bed. They both looked young and innocent.

"Where are you going?" they asked in a chorus.

"Why you want to know?"

"Because we want to go," said Carmen.

"Well, you can't. And now, please leave."

Angel kissed both of the girls on the cheek and pushed them out of the bedroom. She loved her little sister, and was very proud of both of them. Both of the girls were straight-A students.

Once Angel shut the door, the girls knocked on it.

"What, now?"

Lakiyah peeked in and asked, "Can you take us to the mall to-morrow?"

"We'll see. Now, please shut the door."

Angel picked up the remote to her CD player and hit the play button. Aaliyah's *One in a Million* started playing. She hummed along as she thumbed through her wardrobe. *Damn! He could've at least mentioned where he was taking me*, she thought.

"Ooooh!" she squealed. "This is it!"

She had spotted the ideal outfit: her long-sleeve, turtleneck jumpsuit by Ralph Lauren. It had an open front slit, from neck to waist, that would tease any eye with a peek of her voluptuous body. She pulled out her black, T-strap slingbacks by Isaac Mizrahi and her beaded, black Gucci bag. Both were brand-new, still in their boxes. Thank God for her check hustle. She laid the expensive items across her bed as she reminded herself she needed to stop her scamming before she got busted. After she dusted on a little makeup she slid into her jumpsuit.

"Damn, I look good!" she said as she twirled around. She put on her Stephen Dweck earrings, slipped on her shoes, and since she felt cocky, she dabbed on Isabella Rossellini's Manifesto fragrance. Her hair was already in a French roll. All she had to do was bump the bangs. She stood up, looked herself over once more, and blew a kiss to her reflection in the mirror. She turned off the CD player when she heard the buzz of the doorbell and the sound of the girls running to the door. Angel grabbed her Gucci bag and headed for the living room.

Julia, of course, was sitting at her desk doing paperwork. She always brought her work home with her. She noticed her daughter from the corner of her eye, dressed from head to toe. She smelled her perfume before she even came into the living room.

"Why the hell are you wearing so much perfume?"

"I only have on a dab," Angel answered as she bent down and kissed her mom on the cheek.

"Where are we going tonight, and with whom?" Julia asked her daughter.

"I'm not sure."

"Not sure?" Julia turned around and looked at Angel.

"And why is your jumpsuit not zipped up?"

"Ma, this is how it's made."

"How are you going out with a man you don't even know?"

"Mooom," she whined. "He's at the door now. And I do know him."

Carmen and Lakiyah were standing at the door, bombarding Snake with questions.

"Excuse me, ladies." Angel pushed her way between them.

"Come in, Keenan."

She got a whiff of his Armani cologne and he looked mighty GQ-smooth to her. He was wearing a black, V-necked silk sweater and cashmere trousers. Of course, he topped it off with black snakeskin shoes.

"This is my mother, Julia Smith. Mom, this is Keenan High-tower."

"How do you do, ma'am?" He handed Julia a small bouquet of flowers. When she looked up, Julia's heart almost dropped to her feet.

"Aren't you Cleve's son? And you have three uncles, Dino, Stephen, and Monk?" she shot at him.

"Yes, ma'am," he answered with a little hesitancy.

"Well, I grew up with all of them." Julia raised her eyebrows. Her words obviously had a hidden meaning, but Angel had no idea what her mother meant. "How did you meet my daughter?"

"I met her during the lunch hour at the Steak Pub. She dropped all of her books and I helped her pick them up."

"Where do you work?"

"I have a management business. Mostly local talent but it pays the bills."

"Where are you taking my daughter?"

"I have tickets to see Carl Thomas, and I'll be sure to have her home at a respectable hour."

Angel was getting antsy. She grabbed Snake's hand and pulled him toward the door.

"It was a pleasure meeting you, Mrs. Smith," he managed to say before Angel closed the door behind them. Julia didn't bother to answer.

"She's acting like this is my first date," Angel said as they walked to the elevator. "I haven't seen her this nervous over a date since I was in high school. And you think she was bad, you just missed my girlfriends. I don't know what's up with everyone."

"It's probably because all of those men she mentioned are my uncles, and they're pimps," Snake answered directly, without hesitation.

"Pimps!" Angel shrieked. "So you're trying to say that you come from a long line of pimps?"

"Yes, I am."

"Seriously. What do you do?"

"I'm a pimp by blood, not relation." Snake sang Jay-Z's song. Angel started laughing.

"If they're your uncles, then you are related. Do you plan on pimping me?" she joked.

"We'll see." Snake grinned.

"Nigga, you got me twisted." She thought he was still joking.

That night was off the hook. Carl Thomas was the bomb. The restaurant was the bomb. The whole atmosphere couldn't have been more perfect. They vibed very well. Snake loved the fact that Angel had a good head on her shoulders. Angel was even more impressed with him.

After that perfect night, the two were inseparable, even after Angel discovered that Snake really was a pimp, and a cold one at that. Snake kept that side of his life away from Angel. At least most of the time.

One night, Angel watched in horror as he beat his white whore, who everyone called Ice. After that, Angel didn't speak to Snake for almost two weeks. Then on another occasion she saw him beat Big Nell. He broke her jawbone and fractured her rib cage. Once again, she didn't speak to him for several weeks. Each time, Snake would explain to her that, that was the nature of the business, then he'd romance her to death. She always gave in. She couldn't help herself. She was crazy about Snake. He fulfilled all her needs and wants. He paid the rent and looked after the whole family. He even paid her college tuition. Not to mention that the sex was better than any she had ever had. Most importantly, he treated her like a queen and encouraged her to fulfill her dreams.

Julia finally had to accept Snake as a part of their lives. After enough time had passed, she trusted that Snake was not going to turn her daughter out. Whether it was because her daughter was strong-willed or because Snake truly cared about her didn't really matter to Julia. As long as her daughter stayed in law school where she belonged.

And to that end, Julia couldn't deny it was nice having Snake around to help put Angel through school. After so many difficult years, it was good to get some financial help. As long as she didn't think about where the money came from, she was happy to accept Snake's assistance.

It wasn't until everyone was used to Snake's money that he and Angel started beating on each other. Julia hated that they fought so much, but she never pushed the issue with her daughter. The one time she expressed concern, Angel told her not to worry. She could handle her own business. Julia supposed that after so many years in the projects, she was probably right. Angel could handle herself. And after such a long, hard road, Julia was tired. Tired of struggling to stay above water with all the bills. Tired of worrying so much about her remaining children. If Snake could help out with the bills and Angel didn't mind their fights, then Julia was content to sit at her desk and work around the confusion. Life had made Julia numb.

It was in this atmosphere that Angel, the promising law student, became the steady girl of a vicious pimp.

Chapter 8

When Snake and Angel had been seriously dating for a little over a year, he threw her a surprise birthday party. That's when he gave her a big rock and proposed marriage. Even though she was happy about the ring, Angel had some problems with marrying Snake. She told him she could only marry him after he divorced himself from pimping. Snake promised that all he needed was a little time, then he would leave the business and they could get married. Angel was still waiting for Snake to keep that promise.

Snake smiled as he thought about Angel. She was a good woman. Even though she wanted him to leave pimping, she only gave him shit about it once in a while. Most of the time she just let him go on about his business, which was exactly what he planned to do. He parked in front of Club Charlie's; before he got out of the car he sat and watched two of his whores, Raven and Coffey. They both were grabbing on the same man.

"These are some dumb bitches," he mumbled to himself. "All these tricks out here and both of them grabbin' on the same one. They both better have my money when I come back."

Snake eased out of his Benz and slid into the club. The DJ was spinning house music, and the place was packed, as always, even though it was only 7:30. That was the only thing Snake didn't like about the club. It was too damn crowded. Still, he kept coming back because of the food. Rocco, the chef, knew how to hook up some sirloin steak.

As Snake squeezed through the crowd on his way back to his regular table, a few females were trying to get his attention. He didn't have the time right now. He was hungry. Plus Big Nell was sitting there looking agitated.

"Hey, Daddy, are you okay?" She took a long drag on her Newport.

"Naw. I'm fuckin' tensed with the po-po raidin' just about every day. The cash flow ain't been right," Snake complained. "And what's up with that bitch, Holly? She ain't gave me no money in 24 hours. I'm gonna put my foot in her ass when I catch her."

"Holly got picked up yesterday morning." Nell shook her head. "That mean-ass judge wants her to do ninty days. He's tired of seeing her."

Snake leaned back on the cushioned headrest. "See what I mean? One of my hos is gettin' locked up every day and them judges is givin' at least thirty days."

"You hungry?"

Big Nell didn't even wait for an answer. She eased up and went to order Snake's favorite meal—a big, fat, well-done sirloin steak, broccoli and cheese potato soup, and a sourdough roll.

As he sat chillin' and groovin' to the music, Monet, the waitress, brought Snake a scotch on ice. She set it on the table, then leaned over and kissed Snake on the neck.

"What's up, baby? She brushed her breast against his arm. Monet had been trying to get with Snake for a long time, even though she knew she was playing on dangerous ground. She liked him but not enough to be a ho.

"How you doin'?" Snake asked.

"I'm cool."

Just then, Big Nell came back to the table.

"What the fuck do you want?" Nell spat out. Monet ignored her.

"Snake, baby, can I get you anything else?"

"No, I'm a'ight. Thanks, baby."

Monet rolled her eyes at Big Nell and eased her way back through the crowd.

The DJ was spinning "Wifey" by Next as Big Nell set Snake's meal on the table. The aroma of the well-seasoned sirloin was making her stomach growl. She sat down and sipped her "Sex on the Beach," while Snake took his time enjoying his meal.

"You want anything else, Daddy?"

Snake looked up at Big Nell. The years of being a whore were starting to wear on what was once a pretty face. Her eye and nose were still bruised from the ass whipping he'd given her the other night.

"Yeah, I want something else. I want my money, bitch!"

"That's what I wanted to talk to you about." Big Nell's brow was creased with worry. "Please hear me out, Snake. My mother's sick and I need to take off for about a week to find someone to look after her. I need to hold on to the money I got so that I can leave tonight."

"What the fuck did you just tell me?" Snake shouted above the noise of the club. "I run this shit. You ask me permission to leave. You don't fuckin' tell me what you're gonna do."

Snake stood up to grab her. Nell, anticipating the move, crouched back in the corner. He stepped around the table to where she was and tried again to grab her. Nell started kicking both feet like a child.

"Get up!" Big Nell was still crouched in the corner, trembling.

"I'll only be gone for a week."

"Get the fuck up, bitch!"

Snake lunged toward her and tried to grab her arm. Instead, he grabbed her blouse and it ripped open. Her big tits bounced out. If the crowd wasn't looking before, now all eyes were on them, hoping to get a glimpse of the action. Snake grabbed her by her long weave as Nell started screaming. He smacked her across the face with the palm of his hand. She still kept screaming. He hit her hard with the back of his hand. That slap hit her right ear. She thought she was still screaming, but now she couldn't hear anything. Snake didn't let go of her hair as he pulled her toward the door. Big Nell struggled to stay on her feet as she followed Snake. The onlookers made room for this 6-foot 3-inch man, dragging a scantily dressed woman with her tits hanging out.

Outside the club, Snake shoved Nell to make her stand upright. He was ready to punch the life out of her, but she covered her head and crouched down to the ground. Snake started kicking her. Big Nell didn't even move. Her body was almost numb. She laid flat on the ground, looking up into Snake's eyes. This made him even madder. *This bitch won't even fight back*. He started stomping her until the blood gushed from her head, nose, and mouth. Big Nell was no longer conscious. She had released her bowels and lay there in a mixed pool of blood, shit, and piss.

The cool fall breeze took the smell through the air and people in the crowd started covering their noses. Monet, the waitress, started puking. Snake was in his glory. He had an audience. He picked up Nell's foot and dragged her toward the gutter where the sewer was. Her body left a trail of her excrement. Nell's back and arm was raw from being dragged across the cement. Pieces of her flesh lay on the ground. Snake tried to stuff her limp body in the sewer.

The crowd looked on in horror and bewilderment. This was an ass whippin' from hell. Most of the people in there knew about Snake's reputation as the meanest pimp around, and no one had the balls to stop him. Coffey and Raven, who had been outside to witness the whole thing, hugged each other and cried. They were trembling uncontrollably. They knew that their daddy was capable of killing them, but they didn't think he would actually do it. Now their sister Big Nell was gone.

Snake admired his handiwork as he brushed Nell's fluids off his hands and clothes. He could feel the fear in the crowd, and he loved it. He shot a glance at Coffey and Raven.

"I'll see you two in about an hour," he growled at them as he jumped in his car and sped away.

Coffey and Raven ran over to check on Big Nell. They were crying hysterically. The ambulance siren wailed in the distance. Coffey put her trembling fingers on Nell's neck.

"She has a pulse!" she cried.

"Hang in there, baby," Raven whispered.

"Please hang in there."

Chapter 9

Two and a half months later, Big Nell showed up at Snake's apartment. He had already heard over the wire that she was coming back to him. Snake stood in the doorway and looked her up and down.

"Well, well, well. Look what the wind blew in," he said.

"Am I still welcome here, or what?" asked Big Nell with a smile.

Snake stepped aside and motioned her in. He had to admit that she looked good, considering everything that had happened. She had a well-rested look. She looked even better when she handed him two thousand dollars. He stuffed it into his pocket without a word of thanks.

"Hey, Daddy. I'm sorry for taking you through all of that drama," she purred. "But I'm back, and you know I'll work extra hard to make it up to you. Let me clean up and fix your favorite meal."

She kissed Snake on the lips and slid her hands down to squeeze his dick.

"I've really missed you," she said as she gave him another kiss.

Snake didn't answer. He sat down, grabbed the remote and

turned to ESPN. Big Nell went to the kitchen and Snake heard her banging around the pots and pans. It seemed strange having her around again, but Snake wasn't complaining. First of all, the ole girl could cook. Snake knew he would eat well tonight. Plus, she was always a good money maker, and it would be good to have her cash back in his pockets.

After he watched the news, Snake went to take a shower. As he was taking off his shirt Nell came into the bathroom and suggested that he take a relaxing bath instead. She turned on the hot water and let it run real slow. She gave Snake another kiss and started unzipping his pants. Her strong hands ran up and down his long dick, but it was responding slowly. She wondered why he was so tense. She got down on her knees and licked the head lightly. As the licks got more rapid, his dick began to harden and Snake started to moan.

"That feels good, baby."

She slowly put his nine and a half inches into her mouth, a couple of inches going down her throat. They didn't call her Big Nell for nothing. Snake tried to push all 9 1/2 inches in as far as he could get it. It was feeling real good. Nobody ever sucked his dick like Big Nell, not even Angel. His knees and legs got weak as he flowed into her mouth.

"I missed you, Daddy," Nell said, still on her knees. "Go ahead and enjoy your hot bath."

Nell got up and turned off the hot water, then left him alone to enjoy his bath. *Damn, I need to leave a bitch for dead more often*, he thought to himself as he slid into the piping hot water.

When Snake emerged from the bathroom, his meal was laid out on a beautifully set table. Everything was set for a king pimp. Snake inhaled the aroma of his well-done sirloin, covered with mushroom sauce. She hooked up his potato broccoli and cheese soup and pulled the sourdough rolls from the oven. His condo hadn't smelled this good in a long time.

"Sit down and enjoy your meal, baby," she said as she buttered the steaming hot sourdough rolls.

Big Nell sat across from him and smiled as he gobbled down the meal she had so tenderly prepared. He was acting like he hadn't eaten in days.

"How is it, baby?"

"Mm-mm. Very good."

He picked up his glass of Coke, guzzled it down and let out a big belch. As he leaned back and wiped his mouth with a napkin, he took a good look at Big Nell. The skin on her arm was discolored where he had dragged her body across the cement. Her nose was a little crooked.

"Why don't you go watch some more TV?" she suggested after his stare started to make her feel self-conscious.

When Snake stood up from the table, he felt a rush. He turned and started toward the living room, noticing that his body felt very heavy. He sat down on the sofa and laid his head back.

"Damn, baby. I feel tired as hell," he hollered to Nell in the kitchen.

"Go take a nap."

Snake thought about it. A nap sounded so good right about now. He wanted to move, but his body wouldn't go anywhere. He finally forced himself to stand up.

Nell was standing in the kitchen doorway, watching him.

"The fuckin' room is spinning," he said.

"Go lie down, baby. Maybe your bath was just too hot."

Snake had to hold onto the wall as he walked down the hall toward his bedroom. Something was not right, and he was starting to get suspicious.

"What the fuck did you do to me?" He stared at Big Nell, who was standing perfectly still. She offered no help as he stumbled around, bumping into walls. She knew exactly what was wrong with him. All that was left now was for Snake to pass out, and she could complete her plan. But it looked like it would take a little longer than she had expected. He was actually coming toward her, arms outstretched like he thought he could hurt her in the condition he was in. Nell wasn't too afraid that he would actually do any harm, but she wasn't taking any chances with this motherfucker. She backed up slowly.

"What did you put in my food?" He finally reached her and dug his fingers into her arms. His grip was very weak. Nell pushed him off and ran to the closet where she grabbed a baseball bat.

"I put poison in your food, you heartless motherfucker!" she yelled and whacked him across the back.

"Arrgh! You fuckin' bitch!" Snake screamed in agony. Big Nell stepped back and looked at him. She was enjoying the look of pain on his face. "You better kill me," he moaned in agony.

"That's what I plan on doing," she said with a demonic laugh as she cracked the bat over his head. She had no idea what parts of the body she was striking. She just kept pounding away. Tears clouded her vision, but she felt and heard bones cracking as she pounced over and over again, and it made her feel good. Nell was exacting revenge for all the ass whippings she had endured at the hands of Snake, all the times he had made her beg for her life.

But more than all of the physical punishment Snake had inflicted on her, what hurt the most was the fact that she hadn't been able to be by her mother's side when she died. Big Nell was lying unconscious in the hospital on her mother's dying day. She wasn't there for her own mother's funeral. Her folks back home thought she was dead. She didn't even get a chance to tell her mother, "I'm sorry for not turning out the way you wanted me to." The pain of that loss was still tearing at Nell's heart every day. It felt a hundred times worse than the memory of that last beating she got from Snake. Each blow she struck against Snake's body now was payback for what he had done to her.

As she kept pounding on Snake's crushed body, blood was splashing everywhere. Nell was in a frenzy. She kept swinging away, even when there seemed to be no life left in Snake's body. A knock on the door finally snapped her back to reality. She threw the bat down, ran to grab her purse, snatched her two thousand dollars out of Snake's pocket and gave him one last kick. She ran out the back door. Once she was outside and a safe distance from the condo, she fell to the ground and sobbed uncontrollably. She was free now, and so was everyone else.

PART TWO

Kyra

Chapter 10

Angel, her mother, and Kyra had just come from a relative's funeral. Shawn was only twenty-one years old, but he had been shot trying to rob a jewelry store. After the services were over, Kyra drove Angel and Julia home. They pulled up in front of the apartment building, and all three women stepped out of the car. As they stood and talked about the tragedy of Shawn's death, Kyra spotted Tyler's little brother, Lil' Anthony, speeding around in a brand new Camaro. There was no doubt the car was stolen. She waved him down and approached the driver's side window.

"Yo, Kyra." He smiled as he turned down the radio. "What up? You want a ride, or what?"

"Please, Anthony. You know I ain't about to get in no stolen ride. You're playing with fire, you know. Why don't you find yourself another hobby?" Kyra suggested.

"Yeah, whatever." He wasn't interested. Kyra's advice went in one ear and out the other. "Don't you worry bout my hobbies. I got everything under control."

"I'm just worried about you, that's all."

"Just call me if you ever want a ride," Lil' Anthony told her, then turned the music back up. Their conversation was obviously over. Kyra stepped away from the car, and Lil' Anthony pulled off, his squealing tires leaving a black trail on the pavement.

Kyra shook her head as she watched the car disappear in the distance. She was tired of going to funerals for young black men. Too many of them were out there playing dangerous games, ending up like Shawn. Kyra walked back to Angel and Julia. They knew what she was thinking without anyone having to say a word.

"Well, girls, I'm going inside to get out of this dress," Julia told them, then kissed Kyra on the cheek. "Tell your mother to call me."

"I will. Bye, Aunt Julia," Kyra called after her as Julia went into the house.

"Why aren't you coming in?" Angel asked her as she leaned against the door of the Jeep.

"Can't. I'm going to Roz's. Why won't you come with me?" Kyra pleaded. "I need to talk to y'all. It won't take long."

"I don't feel up to it. Do you really need me there?"

"Really, really need you."

Angel thought about it. She looked at Kyra and then back at her house. "This better be important," she said as she jumped back into the Jeep.

"So you're still pissed off because you haven't heard from that tired-ass Snake?"

"I don't know what you see in tired-ass Tyler," Angel snapped back, still not turning away from the window. "He ain't nothing but a ho! You can do better."

"I know I can. That's why I want to talk to y'all."

Angel finally turned and looked at her, but both of them were silent, thinking about their choices in men.

"How could you even fuck him, knowing he has all of them hos?" Kyra broke their silence. Angel sighed, but didn't answer.

"Angel, I know you heard me."

She turned to Kyra. "Condoms. Anyway, he didn't fuck them," Angel said with assurance. "That's what he had me for."

"Puh-leese." Kyra sucked her teeth. "You believe that shit?"

"Why shouldn't I?" Angel asked. "Keenan never gave me any type of infection in two and a half years. I told you before, I get tested every six months for HIV."

"Yeah, but you must've had some doubts if you even felt like you needed to be tested so damn much." Kyra shook her head in disbelief. Her cousin could be so naïve sometimes, and Snake had definitely taken advantage of that. She turned on the radio instead of pressing the issue with Angel.

When they pulled up in front of Roz's, Kyra parked behind Jaz's silver Volkswagen Jetta. The tags on it read 123 JAZ. The sun was shining, but it was a typical cool, crisp autumn day in New Jersey. Angel rang the bell and Roz ran down to open the door.

"What up, y'all?" She smiled, then hugged her girls. "Come on in and get comfortable. I'm serving nonalcoholic wine and crackers."

Angel and Kyra shot each other a glance. Something was up.

"I haven't seen everyone in a while," Roz explained. "Plus, I got a bomb to drop on Kyra."

"Why does it have to be a bomb on me?" Kyra tilted her head to one side and crossed her arms in front of her.

"It's only a bomb if you let it be a bomb," said Jaz as she came out of the kitchen. She was wearing a mocha dress that matched her skin tone. It looked like she was wearing a slip.

"Why are you dressed like that?" Kyra asked.

"I have a date with Faheem. And for your info, this is a Dolce

& Gabbana," Jaz bragged as she did a turn to show them the back. "Eight hundred and fifty dollars."

"Whatever," Kyra replied. "So Faheem finally quit slangin'?"

"I could have gotten you that dress for half price," Angel announced, but Jaz ignored her and answered Kyra.

"Yeah. It's on like popcorn. But let's not go into that. I'm here to hear this announcement you have to make, then I'm gonna say what I gotta say, and then I'm out." Jaz pushed up her chest so her cleavage practically spilled out of the tight dress.

They were all seated on the living room sofa. Kyra made her announcement first.

"I got promoted to assistant to the head psychologist. I'll be making an extra $14,000 a year. And I have a job as soon as I graduate."

"What? That's the bomb!" Angel clapped her hands.

"Hell, yeah," Jaz and Roz agreed, giving each other high fives.

"We're on course, ladies. We are not gonna let the hood take us under," said Angel. "Let's toast."

"Wait! Wait! That's not all," Kyra continued. "I'm leaving Tyler and moving to New Brunswick."

"Wait a minute." Angel looked at her. "Why do you have to move?"

"New job. New beginning. Drop old habits. I can't be a doctor shacking up with a drug dealer. I'll lose my license if something goes down. Plus, I know he's fuckin' around on me. He sure ain't fuckin' me."

Everybody got quiet.

"Well, you know that nigga ain't gonna let you just up and leave without a fight," Angel reminded her.

"Yeah, I know. I still got love for the brother. But a sister gots to move on."

"You're just going to up and leave your apartment?" Angel asked.

"Fuck the apartment. What about up and leaving an eight-year relationship?" asked Jaz.

"It's not my apartment. Its Tyler's. And as far as the relationship goes, I'm just not feeling it."

"Well, since we're on the subject," Roz chimed in, "remember I said I got a bomb for you? Tyler and that apartment are the least of your worries."

All eyes were on Roz as she continued. "Marvin's home from his seven-year bid, and he's been looking for you."

Everybody gasped. Kyra sank back into the sofa. Her stomach started doing flips. "Bitch, don't play like that."

"I ain't playin'. Go ask my aunt. You forgot she works at the parole office?"

"Damn! Damn! Damn!" Kyra buried her face in her hands. The whole room got quiet. Marvin was a memory they had all tried to bury and forget. They vowed long ago that they would allow no one or nothing to take them down. Marvin had almost succeeded at doing just that.

"So what are you going to do?" Roz asked, hands on her hips.

Kyra stood up and grabbed her purse. Her knees felt weak. She definitely was not ready for this hurdle. The shit was about to hit the fan and she wanted to be far away when it started to fly.

"I'll catch y'all later." She headed out the door before they could say anything.

Chapter 11

Kyra jumped into her Jeep, stirred her vanilla cappuccino and set it in the cup holder. She opened the cinnamon granola bar, broke it into little pieces, and set them in a napkin. After she checked her mirrors, she turned on the radio to 98.7 KISS. "Always and Forever" was playing.

"Is this supposed to be a fuckin' sign?" she said out loud as she pulled away from the rest stop. She had to laugh. That song took her way back. All the way to the 9th grade.

It was the second day of school, and Kyra was the only one in the crew who didn't have a boyfriend. Roz, Jaz, and Kyra were standing around the lockers, trying to look cute while they waited for the first-period bell to ring. Kyra looked up and grinned when she saw a cutie coming up the hall toward them. He was fine, clean, and had that playa's walk. Kyra's heart was beating a mile per minute. She had to work hard to keep her cool.

"Damn! Who is that?" She wanted to know right then and there.

"That's Tyler Dawson. He lives down the street from me," said Jaz. "He got five or six brothers, and all of them got it goin' on."

Kyra walked over to Tyler and snatched his schedule out of his hand.

"What section are you in?" she asked as she examined the info on the tattered piece of paper.

Tyler looked at her like she was crazy. He looked at her friends, who were looking at each other, eyes wide. Kyra wasn't usually so forward. It dawned on Tyler that this honey was trying to get her mac on. "What section are *you* in?"

"I'm in 9-1. I'm always at the top of my game," Kyra bragged.

"Oh, you're one of them braniacs, huh?"

"Hey, what can I say?"

"What's your name?"

"Kyra."

"What's yours?"

"Ty."

Just then the bell rang. They stood looking at each other.

"C'mon!" Jaz hollered.

"I'll see you around." Kyra smiled as she turned and waltzed away. She was in love. So was he. He stood there and watched her until she turned the corner.

"Dang, Kyra, you was all over him," Roz said.

"Hell, yeah!" Jaz chimed in. "You embarrassed the hell out of us."

They all started laughing.

"I couldn't help it, y'all." Kyra blushed.

Kyra immediately went to work investigating Tyler's background. How old was he, who he hung out with, did he have a girlfriend, what school did he go to before this one. By the end of the day, she had a full report on her soon-to-be boo. Kyra was very excited about what she dug up.

First of all, at her junior high school, the higher the number after your grade, the dumber you were. Being that he was in 9-8 he wasn't that bright, she assumed. Which was okay by Kyra, because it seemed that all the fine playas were in the not-so-bright classes. Next, he smoked cigarettes. Wow! A real ruff neck. He smoked weed, drank wine and beer. He was supposed to be in the tenth grade and had been locked up before. He rolled with all the playas. Did Kyra care? Hell, no! It was on. He was just what Kyra was looking for. A bad boy!

The next time Kyra saw Ty was at an old school basement house party that one of the high school kids was giving. Even though Kyra and her crew were in junior high, they made sure they hung with the seniors. Kyra, Angel, Roz, and Jaz were in full effect, jammin' and showing off. The dimly lit purple room reeked of sandalwood incense and weed. They all wore tight jeans and T-shirts, and were draped in gold.

"Slow it down!" some horny brother yelled.

"Yeah!" Another horny brother seconded the request.

The DJ knew exactly what to do. He played " Always and Forever" by Heat Wave. The couples took to the floor a little before midnight.

"I'm ready to go, y'all," Jaz announced. Roz and Angel agreed.

"Y'all go ahead. I'ma stay here and get Ty to walk me home," Kyra told them.

"A'ight, cool." They said their good-byes, and then Kyra was left at the party by herself.

Someone passed Kyra a joint as she stood and watched the dance floor. Dudes were coming over, asking her to dance, but she turned them all down. There was only one person she planned on dancing with. She was waiting on Ty to ask her. When she saw him easing toward her, her heart started to flutter and she could barely breathe.

BAM! There he was, standing right in front of her, extending his hand. She reached out and took it, following him to the dance floor. He took her in his arms and held her close. Kyra melted in his arms. As the record ended, Kyra started seeing dark spots. She figured it was because she was nervous as hell. Ty said he wanted to get to know her better and asked her if he could walk her home. Of course she said yes. Everything was going as planned.

After they exchanged numbers, they sat down on a couch in the corner. Kyra could hardly see, and she was sweating like she was in a steam room. Ty went to find her something cool to drink. When he came back, Kyra was passed out on the couch, surrounded by about seven high school dudes. They were looking down at her, talking and arguing.

"Yo, what up, niggas?" Ty asked.

"We getting ready to pull a train on this bitch." The smallest and skinniest dude in the group was all excited. He grinned, gold teeth gleaming.

"What!" Ty's voice went up a couple of notches. He started shaking Kyra. He had done his research, too. He knew she was a virgin, and if anybody was going to get it first, it was gonna be him.

"What the fuck you doing, man?" Rat, the leader of the crew asked. "We gettin' ready to handle our business. This bitch done smoked my weed, and now she got to pay up."

"Yeah!" hollered his sidekick, Yuno, who already had his dick out.

"This is mines, and ain't none of y'all gettin' ready to do shit," Ty announced as he pulled out his gat and cocked it. *Damn*, he said to himself. *Here I am on the other side of town with no backup.*

"Oh, so it's like that?" Rat growled.

"Yeah, it's like that," Ty answered. "Here's ten dollars. Go buy another bag of weed." He threw the money on the floor. Two of the fools dove to pick it up. Rat kicked the one with the money in the stomach and told him to give up the cash.

"Stay your ass on your side of the hood," Rat warned Ty. He turned to walk away, his boys following behind. Yuno looked pissed as he stuffed his dick back in his pants.

Ty knew he had to get his ass out of there. He bent over and shook Kyra hard, trying to wake her up. It took a while, but she finally sat up. She was still groggy, and from the look on her face, Ty knew she had no idea where she even was. He dragged her outside so they could catch a cab.

"Whew! That was fuckin' close," he said. As far as Kyra was concerned, she had just found her knight in bad boy's armor.

Chapter 12

That following Monday at school, Angel, Roz, and Jaz couldn't believe what happened Saturday night at the party. If they would have hung around just a few more minutes, they would have been there for their girl Kyra. Ty was the man in their eyes. It was all over the school how Kyra had almost gotten gang raped until Ty pulled out his gat and chumped all those punks. The females were sweatin' Ty and he was loving every minute of it. They were practically throwing pussy at him. It was very tempting, but Ty was on a mission. A mission called Kyra. He was determined to be the first to bust that cherry.

He and Kyra were spending every day after school together. He would walk her home after school and wouldn't leave her house until about 10:00 every night. They were diggin' each other. After about a month, Ty invited Kyra to come over to his house. She knew that was eventually coming. She also knew that if she wanted to keep a nigga like Ty she would have to give up the pussy. There were no ifs, ands, or buts about it. She was surprised that she'd been able to hold him off this long.

Kyra lost her virginity in Ty's twin bed. It was so quick she

71

didn't even take her bra off, but at least there wasn't as much pain as she anticipated. Ty wore a condom and joked that it came off and was still inside her vagina. She started to panic until he told her he was only playing. They washed up, put on their clothes and went back to school. Kyra was officially a woman now.

From that day on, Ty and Kyra were in love. They would have sex as often as Kyra would sneak out of Study Hall, which ran into her lunch period. Ty would make sure his mom and her boyfriend were both at work, and he'd wait on Kyra. One day they had just finished and gotten dressed when his mother's boyfriend came into the house and went straight upstairs to Ty's room. That was a close call. It was as if he knew Ty had a girl up in his bedroom.

Having sex had Kyra feeling more mature, sexy, and confident. In other words, she was becoming a hot ass. At the age of fourteen, her body was starting to fill out. Her boobs and ass were getting rounder, and her fuck-me attitude was becoming very noticeable to the older dudes hanging on the corner. Every day as she passed the corner with Ty or by herself, the niggas would pause the crap game and flirt with Kyra. On the days when she was by herself, this dude named Marvin would stop what he was doing to walk her the rest of the way home.

"You're my little girlfriend. You know that, don't you?"

"You're too old for me."

"I'm gonna wait for you." He would tell her that every time he saw her.

Marvin was too cute. He was tall, slim, brown-skinned, with big eyes and long, pretty eyelashes. He had a cute, sly smile, and he would give her money and bags of weed, reminding her that when she got a little older, she was going to be his woman. Kyra liked the extra attention, even though her relationship with Ty was going along just fine. Her only complaint was that the sex was getting boring. She was tired of having to sneak in and out of his house and then rush while they were doing it. She wanted to be able to lie there, hug and kiss and just talk while they were naked. Plus, she wanted someone with more experience and with a bigger dick. Ty's dick didn't even hardly feel like anything was inside her.

Something had to change. Kyra was getting bored, and peer pressure was kicking in. She would sit and listen to Kyra's older sister Meka and her best friend Sharon talk about how big their boyfriends' dicks were, and how they tasted like candy. They said their boyfriends would eat their pussies to make them come over and over. Kyra never came. Hearing all that made Kyra very, very curious. All she could expect from Ty was some grinds and kisses for foreplay, then he would put his dick in and hump around for a few minutes before he would come. Those few minutes felt good, but he was only breaking her off a slice. She wanted the whole pie.

One night, Marvin showed up at her door. He was high as a kite.

"What are you doin', coming to my house?" she asked him. She was glad no one was home.

"Calm down, baby girl," he said in his sexy voice. "I just wanted to drop off a bag of this weed for you. It's the shit."

Kyra smiled when she saw the bag he was holding. She opened the door a little wider, and he came into the house.

"You can't stay long, you know," she told him. She reached out for the bag, but he snatched it away with a sly smile.

"Just go get me some paper so I can roll me one, then I'll get ghost."

Kyra didn't waste any time going to get the paper. She was glad Marvin was hooking her up, but she really wanted him out of there fast. Ty was coming over. Even if he was boring her to death these days, she did not feel like explaining to him, or anyone else, why this 22-year-old dude was in her house. She came back to the living room, and Marvin was on the couch. She handed him the papers and watched him roll a joint on her mother's coffee table. *Damn! He sure smells good*, she said to herself. Once he finished rolling, Marvin did like he promised and got up to leave.

As Kyra opened the door for him, Marvin turned around and put his mouth onto hers, circling his tongue around. His hands went into her shorts and he started fingering her. It felt so good, it scared Kyra to death. She pulled away and her whole body was hot and trembling. Marvin smiled at her and left without saying a word.

Later on, when Ty came over, she didn't tell him that Marvin stopped by. They smoked some Hawaiian Gold and just chilled. But Kyra couldn't shake the delicious feeling that Marvin had sent all over her body. Now, that was the shit!

She couldn't wait to tell Angel, Roz, and Jaz about what happened. Especially about how good it felt and how she couldn't stop thinking about him even while Ty was sitting right next to her.

"He's too old for you." Angel said. "Plus, I don't trust him 'cause he always looks high."

"We always high." Kyra tried to defend him.

"Hell, yeah. But I think he be high off of something other than weed," Roz said.

"Like what?"

"I don't know, but it ain't coke because he too laid back."

"He's fine as hell, that's for sho," said Jaz.

"I know. I heard my sister and her friends talking about how they would love to ride his dick," chimed in Roz.

"Well, them bitches can forget it!" Kyra said, marking her territory.

"What about Ty?" asked Jaz.

"Fuck Ty!" said Angel. "My cuz trying to get with the big dicks!" They all burst out laughing while giving each other pounds.

Chapter 13

Once Marvin started buying her little presents, Kyra couldn't keep her mind off him. He'd show up with the gifts—a blouse, earrings, whatever he found that he thought would look good on his little girlfriend, as he still called her. And of course, he still kept her supplied with weed. Even though she was a little scared by their age difference, his attention was thrilling. And it was making her lose interest in everything about Ty.

Sex with Ty had become even more boring. He would lay on top of her, humping away like it was the best sex anyone had ever had. Kyra would lie perfectly still and let him do him. She hardly even faked any noises for him anymore. She was too busy daydreaming about Marvin and what gift he might bring her next. Ty had no idea anything had changed.

One hot summer day, Kyra was going to see Roz. They had planned to go to Jaz's, who was having a party for her cousin Keesha. Kyra was taking the shortcut through the Roger Gardens projects when Marvin spotted her.

"Hey, Kyra!"

She turned around, stopped and waved. Marvin was looking fine, as usual. He looked like he had just come from the barbershop and he had on all white. A white Nike shirt, white Nike shorts, white Nike socks and white Nike sneakers.

"What's up?" She licked her lips.

"Where you going?" he asked.

"To see my homegirl. Where you going, dressed all fly?"

"To find you."

"Why are you trying to find me?" Her heart was fluttering.

"I want us to be twins today."

"And how is that?"

"I got you the same outfit I got on."

"Where is it?" she asked, trying to hide her excitement.

"At the crib. If you ain't scared you can walk over there with me."

"I ain't scared of you."

"Well, come on, then."

They walked in silence for the two blocks to Marvin's apartment. Kyra couldn't believe that she was alone with the man she couldn't stop thinking about. She couldn't wait to get her new outfit.

Marvin lived on the second floor. When he put the key in the door, Kyra heard a dog bark.

"You got a dog?"

"It's just a terrier. He's cool."

"Well, I hope he don't try to bite me." She folded her arms.

"He will if I tell him to."

"Well, I'm not giving him that chance. I'll catch you some other time." She turned to walk away.

"I'm only playin'." Marvin laughed as he grabbed Kyra's arm. "You know I ain't gonna let nothing happen to my baby girl."

"Don't be playing with me like that."

As soon as he opened the door, Marvin grabbed the little terrier and took him in the back. Kyra looked around the living room. She liked what she saw. He had burgundy carpet, burgundy leather furniture, a big screen TV and a phat sound system. She was impressed by a large, sparkling clean fish tank, until she got closer and saw how ugly the fish were.

She walked into the kitchen. It was tiny, but cute and clean. Marvin came in and went to the refrigerator. He was carrying a Foot Locker shopping bag.

"You want a soda or somethin'?" he asked as he handed her the shopping bag.

"No, I'm straight. I want to see what's in the bag." She was already opening it, taking everything out. "Hell, yeah! These are all that!" She was shouting like a kid at Christmastime.

"Go in the bathroom and try everything on."

She grabbed everything and ran into the bathroom. When she came out, she was grinning and spinning around.

"How did you know my size?"

"This ain't my first time buying you somethin'. How quickly we forget!"

"Mmm-hmm." She bent over to fix the Nike socks to fall right above the Nike tennis shoes.

The Nike shorts were tight, just like Marvin had wanted. They showed off her small curves.

"Jailbait!" Marvin said under his breath. Kyra heard him, but pretended she hadn't.

"How do I look?" Kyra asked, twirling around.

"Fine, and sexy as hell."

Kyra blushed. "Don't I know it! What you got good?"

"Look in the ashtray on top of the stereo. There should be something already rolled."

Kyra got the ashtray and lit up a joint. "Do you mind if I turn on your stereo?"

"Go ahead—do whatever you want." Marvin smiled before he

disappeared. Kyra turned on the CD player and hit the play button. He had Isaac Hayes's *Shaft* soundtrack loaded. Kyra thought she was the only one who knew about the soundtrack. It was sounding good, so she danced around his living room for at least ten minutes. When he finally came back, Kyra knew something was up.

"What did you just have?" she asked.

"What do you mean, what did I just have?" He grinned.

"You sure wasn't back there smoking no joint."

"Somethin' you can't handle."

"How do you know what I can't handle?"

"Because you're my baby girl."

"Shit. I ain't no baby girl. I'm grown." Marvin just stared at her.

"Why are you staring at me like that?"

"All right, then. Come over here," he finally answered.

Kyra stood up and approached him as he opened a drawer behind the bar and took out some foil. He set it on the counter. She looked on with curiosity as he put some of the white powder on the edge of a matchbook and sucked it up through his nose.

"Is that coke or heroin?" She asked.

"Oh, you do know a little somethin', huh, baby girl? It's heroin, but we call it *H*," he explained as he put a little on the matchbook cover and passed it to her.

Kyra sniffed it and choked.

"You all right, baby girl?"

"Yeah." Her eyes filled up with water as she sat on the couch and rested her head back. She felt like she was riding up and down on a seesaw and her stomach was getting queasy. It was a funny feeling, sickening but very relaxing. She felt like she was dreaming.

Marvin went to the kitchen, got her a 7-Up, and poured it on some ice.

"Drink a little of this."

Kyra felt like everything was in slow motion as she drank it down.

"Damn, I feel good." She grinned at Marvin.

"Don't ask for no more, okay? I can't have my baby girl strung out." He kissed her on the forehead.

"I'm grown, remember?"

"You know I'm crazy about your wanna-be grown ass, don't you?"

"Crazy in what way? I thought we was just friends. Plus, you know I got a man," Kyra teased.

"Shit. He ain't no fuckin' man. I bet he never even made you come, did he?"

"I'm not telling you our personal business."

"That's because he didn't," Marvin said as he reached over and started massaging her breast.

Kyra just stared at him. He was making her feel higher than she already was. He leaned over and put his tongue in her mouth and circled it around. Kyra's breathing was starting to get heavy as she kissed him back, enjoying the feel of his hands roaming over her body. He gently pushed her back so that she was lying down. As he pulled her shorts down he was giving the inside of her thighs gentle, soft kisses. Kyra felt like she was melting into the leather sofa. The "H" that she had just sniffed magnified every single thing that he did. He pulled off her shirt and un-snapped her bra. Her young, perky tits were a sight for sore eyes.

"I told you that I'm crazy about you. How do you feel about me?"

"I think you are a fine-ass nigga who is too old for me."

"Well, do you want me to stop?" He asked her as he started to gently bite her nipples.

"Unh-uh. Don't stop," she moaned.

The more he bit her nipples and sucked on them, the hotter her pussy juices got and the wetter her panties became. Kyra wanted more. As if he heard her thoughts, Marvin slid her panties down and spread her legs wide so that he could admire her young pussy. Kyra could hardly contain herself. Tyler had never, ever made her feel like this. He had never taken this much time with her.

"Finger me like you did that time at my house," she begged.

"Oh, you liked that, didn't you? I knew you did, 'cause your whole body was trembling. But I got somethin' better than that, baby girl. He spread the lips of her pussy and ran his tongue over her clit.

"Oooh! She moaned loudly. "That feels so good."

Marvin sucked on her clitoris and it got harder and harder. Kyra's moaning got louder. She started circling her hips in a grinding motion. Marvin kept licking, and slipped a couple of fingers into her, working them in and out of her pussy. She felt as if she were rising up out of her body. Then it felt like she was having spasms and her body started to shake uncontrollably. The more her body shook, the faster he licked and moved his fingers in and out. She came for what felt like an eternity and then she blacked out.

Marvin stood up, looking down at Kyra lying there, and was proud of his handiwork. He didn't even use his dick yet and she had already nutted and was knocked out. That's why he really liked the young girls. He could showcase his skills. Plus, he really liked Kyra. He'd been wanting to fuck her for a long time. Her pussy tasted real good. Just as he imagined it would.

He got a towel and dried up the wetness on his leather sofa. Then he took off all his clothes and took another sniff of "H." Kyra was beginning to wake up.

"You okay, baby girl?" He sat down beside her.

Kyra gave a weak smile and he started giving her soft kisses on the lips. She wrapped her arms around his neck and put her tongue in his mouth. Marvin's dick was now good and hard. He inserted two fingers into her pussy and started to move them around, in and out. Kyra raised up both of her knees and started grinding on his fingers.

"Oh, baby, that feels so good," she moaned.

"How good?" he teased.

"Real good."

Her pussy was so wet the juices were pouring out. *This is just the way I like it*, he said to himself. He pulled his fingers out and told her to leave her knees up. He grabbed his dick and squeezed it at the base, causing it to look big and fat. When Kyra looked down at it, her eyes widened.

"Marvin, where do you think you're putting that?"

"Where it belongs. I'll be gentle." He started easing it in nice and slow. Kyra moaned, but it was feeling so good. When he got it in as deep as it would go, she tensed up.

"Relax, baby girl," he whispered into her ear as he made slow, deep, rhythmic moves to stretch the tightness. He kissed her and told her how long he'd waited for this and how good it felt. Kyra was moaning, groaning, and holding on tight. She had never felt like this before. She wrapped her legs around his back, and he responded by moving faster and deeper. Kyra was now hollering and trembling.

"See, baby girl. I told you, you ain't have no man. A fine young sister like you is supposed to get fucked like this all the time. This is my pussy now, and I'm gonna take good care of it," he whispered in her ear.

Kyra was getting ready to come again. *Damn, I should have put on a rubber*, he thought. *This is definitely jailbait*. As much as he wanted to let loose inside her, he knew he couldn't get her pregnant. As she screamed in ecstasy, Marvin had to be still and bite his lip to keep from coming with her. When her young body stopped jerking, he quickly pulled out. Kyra was knocked out again.

Marvin kissed her, got up and went to his stash. He took another snort and then went to take a shower. He dried off and came back into the living room where he'd left his Nike gear. Kyra was stirring. He leaned over and kissed her on the mouth.

"There's clean linen in the bathroom. Go shower so we can go out."

Kyra slowly got up, grabbed her clothes and went into the bathroom. As she showered, she couldn't believe what had just happened. She told herself, *I just snorted some heroin, fucked a grown-ass man and now I'm in his shower. I don't even feel guilty. That shit felt good as hell.* She smiled to herself. After she dried off and lotioned up, she put her clothes on and went out into the living room.

"Where are we going?"

"To Cadwalder Park. We look damn good in these Nike whites. It's corny as hell to be dressed alike, but I don't give a fuck. I want to show you off. Look at that ass in them shorts."

Kyra blushed. What Marvin didn't tell her was that he needed to get to the park to sell some dope. He also wanted to hold onto her because he planned on fucking her again later on. Just the thought of hittin' it again made his dick jump.

"Come here," he said. "Give me a kiss."

Kyra did as he said. He grabbed her and pulled her up close. She felt his hard dick against her and started moving up and down on it real subtle. She was starting to get wet all over again. He pushed her back and said, "You know this pussy is mines, right?"

Kyra nodded. She was breathing hard. She just wanted to get back on his dick again.

"This means you can't be fucking that little boy no more. You understand?"

"Yeah, I understand."

"No more playing house with that little boy."

"I heard you!" she said as she kissed him and positioned herself on that hard dick that she done fell in love with. He kissed her back and then slapped her on the butt.

"If you keep that up I'm gonna have to get me some more of this pussy right now, but I got to take care of some business. You want another hit before we go?"

Disappointed that she couldn't get her groove on, she mumbled, "Might as well."

"Oh, don't worry, baby girl. As soon as I finish handling my business, we're coming back. I gots to get me some more of this."

Kyra smiled as he passed her the matchbook that held the white powder. She sniffed it, and just like the last hit, the water welled up in her eyes. She had to sit on the couch and rest her head back. She was riding on the seesaw again.

Marvin went to the back to get his stash and let the terrier out. He started barking and ran straight to Kyra.

"She's cool, man." Marvin said to his dog.

Kyra paid the dog no attention. Marvin reached over and took her hand.

"Come on, baby girl. Let's go."

Chapter 14

Marvin and Kyra cruised down Stuyvesant Avenue in his souped-up Mustang convertible. The top was down because it was about 80 degrees. It was a gorgeous day and Kyra was feeling nice. The "H" was most definitely a better high than weed. She was liking it a lot.

As they turned into Cadwalder Park, Kyra noticed that everybody and their mama must be out. It was jam-packed as they crept along at five miles an hour. Boom boxes and car stereos were rocking. Folks were just chilling. Males were hollering at Marvin and the females were trying to figure out who he had in the car. They found a parking spot and got out to walk around.

"Kyra!" someone shouted. Kyra turned around to see who it was. "Over here!" Lulu came walking toward her, sipping on a wine cooler. Lulu was fourteen, just like Kyra, and also thought she was grown. Lulu was a beautiful Puerto Rican girl, but she was nosy and talked too much.

"*¿Qué pasa?*" Kyra said, trying to practice her Spanish. Just as she hugged Lulu, Marvin told Kyra to stay put. He said he'd be back in a New York minute.

"Ain't that Marvin, girl?" Lulu sounded excited and jealous at the same time.

"Yeah, that's him."

"Ooh, la la la!" Lulu said, clicking her tongue. "He is fine as hell. Ain't he bout 25 or 26?"

"No, he's 22."

"What's up with you and Tyler?"

Kyra knew that was coming. "Ain't nothin' up no more, Lulu."

"Whaaaat?" Lulu stretched out the word.

Just then, Marvin called her. "Thank God," Kyra said under her breath. "Her big mouth, 20-questions-asking ass was about to blow my high."

"I'll catch you later, Lulu," Kyra said as she ran to catch up with Marvin. She knew that Lulu couldn't wait to run her mouth about Kyra being with Marvin.

Kyra and Marvin strolled through the park in their matching white outfits. People were definitely noticing them, and Kyra felt proud. Marvin told her how fly she looked and bought her some ice cream. She sat on a bench and waited for him while he sold more dope.

"What up, Kyra?" hollered Joe, one of Tyler's friends. She waved and kept on licking her ice cream cone. She was running into all of Tyler's friends. But at least that was better than running into him. Marvin came back to get her.

"Come on, baby girl, let's go get something to eat." She liked it when he called her baby girl.

"Okay," she said gladly. She wanted to leave before her luck ran out and she saw Tyler. She knew his homies would run back and tell him that they saw her and who she was with. Just as they reached the car another voice hollered.

"What up, Kyra?" It was Chuck, another one of Ty's boys. He grabbed her and hugged her. "Where's Ty?"

"He ain't here, motherfucker! Now, get the fuck out her face!" Marvin glared at Chuck. Chuck didn't even say anything. He just looked at him and walked away. Kyra started laughing.

Kyra was enjoying her day. The Ground Round was where all the playas hung out. The playas took it over. They hung out, they transacted their business, they ate, drank, and smoked weed. After they left the "Round"—as everyone called it—Marvin took her back to the apartment where they got high and had sex again. This time he made sure he wore some protection. Kyra enjoyed it even more because they were in his king-size brass bed and she came three times before they both fell asleep. When Kyra rolled over and looked at the clock a while later, it read 12:17.

"Shit!" She jumped up. "My mom is going to kill me." She shook Marvin to wake him and told him he had to hurry up and get her home. Marvin did not want to get out of bed, but he knew this was the price he would have to pay for dealing with such a young girl. They got dressed, and he drove her home. He parked a block away so none of her nosy-ass neighbors would see her getting out of his ride. Marvin kissed her and promised to hook up with her the next day.

Kyra was relieved that she was able to sneak into the house unnoticed. Everything was quiet. No Moms waiting up for her, ready to whip her ass. When she looked around the house, she saw that no one was even home. She laughed at herself as she turned on the hall light. Her high was beginning to wear off, and the only thing she wanted to do was soak in some hot water and jump in the bed. As she relaxed in her hot, bubbly tub she couldn't believe what had happened today. She'd woken up with intentions of going over to Roz's to hang out until later on. Then they would go over to Jaz's, because she was throwing a party for her cousin Keesha. But instead, her plans got sent in another direction. Instead, she got fucked real good by a grown-ass man, had five orgasms, and sniffed some dope. The scary thing was, she had no regrets. The only thing that was nagging her was going through the drama of breaking it off with Tyler. She knew he was whipped and was not going to let her go just that easy. She liked Tyler a lot. He'd saved her from getting gang raped, but it was time to move on to bigger and more mature things. She got out of the tub, dried off, put on her pajamas and fell asleep as soon as her head hit the pillow.

The next morning, Kyra's brother hit her in the back with the phone. She sat up and called him a fag.

"The phone's for you, you dummy!" Darren said.

Fuck you, she mouthed, just in case her mother was within earshot.

She looked at her clock. It was 11:48 A.M.

"What!" She spoke into the mouthpiece, still not fully awake.

"What the fuck happened to you yesterday?" It was Roz, and she heard Angel laughing in the background, so that meant they were on three-way.

"You called and said you were on your way over. We waited and waited and you never showed. Jaz is mad at you because you knew she was giving Keesha a party and you didn't even show up."

"Yeah," chimed in Angel. "Tyler was there, messing up everybody's groove, 'cause you wasn't there. He kept acting like we knew where you was. I was 'bout to slap him. We heard you was rolling with that dope dealer Marvin. Speak up, bitch! We want the 411 and we want it now!"

"Why y'all gotta be waking me up asking so many damn questions? It's only—"

Angel cut her off. "Just state the facts. We want to know. Did you fuck him?"

Kyra was quiet, but grinning.

"Ooooooh!" They both sang it like it was a duet.

"You fucked a grown man?" Roz shrieked in disbelief.

Kyra tried to remain quiet, but couldn't hold it in any longer. "Yeah, I did. And guess what?"

"What?" they both hollered at the same time with their ears glued to the phone.

"I had five orgasms!" She was trembling at the memory.

"You lying bitch!" Angel said.

"No, I am not lying. You know how long I've been complaining about not having one. Well, yesterday I had two on his couch, and then when we came back later that night, I had three in the bed."

"Damn! He's that good?" asked Roz.

"Yes, he is, girl! I am in love! He even ate me out."

"Ooh, you nasty!" Angel said.

"It felt so good. Tyler ain't got shit on Marvin."

Kyra told them everything. The matching white Nike outfits. How the bitches were jealous because she was looking too good. The older girls were all in his face but he wasn't giving them no play. She told them how big-mouth Lulu and then Tyler's boys was all in her face. They all laughed when she told them how Marvin had to step to stupid-ass Chuck.

"You know he sells dope, don't you?" Angel asked.

"How do you know?" Kyra was being sarcastic.

"Just don't say I ain't tell you. Seriously, I just want you to be careful," Angel warned her.

Kyra decided not to tell them she snorted some powder. She would never hear the end of it.

"I gotta go, y'all," Kyra said.

"You coming over?" asked Roz.

"Marvin's coming to pick me up about 2:00. I gotta do my

hair, shower and clean up before my mom starts fussin'. Plus, I want to get out of here before Tyler comes. I know he's too mad to call."

"Yeah, he was pissed last night. He thinks you was fucking around on him," Roz said.

"You think so?" asked Kyra.

"Yup. He ain't stupid," Angel said. "You won't be able to hide from the brother forever."

"Fuck it! Be a playa-playa and keep both of them," Roz suggested.

"Shit. Marvin told me to stop fucking Ty and dump his ass ASAP."

"What? That's what he said?" Angel asked.

"Hell, yeah. I can't even play him. I could prob'ly play Ty, but Marvin would kick my ass. I'll call y'all tonight. Peace out!" Kyra hung up the phone to get ready for Marvin.

Chapter 15

Kyra did her house chores, did her hair and got dressed. She put on a white Nike tennis dress to match the white Nike tennis shoes Marvin had given her. It was very short and looked hot on her. You couldn't tell her she wasn't all that. It was almost 2:30 and Marvin hadn't showed.

Damn! she thought. *He could've at least called.* She was anxious and fidgety, so she decided to walk up to the corner ice cream shop.

It was another gorgeous day out, just like yesterday. Kyra was looking forward to another day with Marvin. As she neared the corner, there was a bunch of niggas hangin' out, but Marvin wasn't among them.

"Damn!" she said out loud.

"What's the matter, baby girl?" asked Rock, Marvin's partner and one of the regulars on the corner. "You looking for my boy Marv?"

"Hell, no. I ain't looking for Marvin." She rolled her eyes at Rock. She couldn't help but notice he was fine as hell, too. Little did she know Marvin done already spread the word that he got that on lock. Baby Girl was off-limits.

Rock smiled, ignoring her comment. "He went out on the east side. He should be back in an hour."

Kyra went inside the Stuyvesant Ice Cream Parlor. She looked over the ice cream, not really wanting to taste anything but Marvin. She ended up playing Street Fighter just to kill some more time. Plus, it was nice and cool inside. When she did finally step outside, she didn't notice Tyler coming up the street.

"Yo, Kyra!" he called.

Oh, shit! She said to herself. She could tell by the look on his face that he was still pissed off. *I might as well get it over with so I can enjoy the rest of my day.*

"Where you been, Kyra? I came over your house twice and I kept calling. And don't tell me you was at no party, 'cause I stayed there until midnight." Tyler was heated. "And why the fuck were you in the park with that nigga Marvin? What's up with you, Kyra?"

Folks were starting to gather near them because it sounded like something was getting ready to jump off.

"Look, Tyler, it's over between me and you. "It—"

He cut her off. "What the fuck you mean it's over? How you gonna just walk away just like that? No fuckin' explanation, no—"

Now she was heated. "Don't be cussing at me, Tyler. It's over. What part don't you fuckin' understand, the 'it's' or the 'over'?"

"Oh, you sound like that nigga done already hit it. Did he hit it, Kyra?" Tyler was screaming.

"Well, you damn sure ain't hittin' it!" she screamed back at him and turned to walk away.

Tyler came up behind her and grabbed her arm. Kyra yanked away from his grip. Marvin's crew, Snail and Rock, came and stood in front of Tyler. Kyra kept walking.

"Look, man, chill," Snail told him. "Let it go, man."

"Why you all up in mines, nigga? You don't know me," Tyler said, all up in Snail's face.

Rock pulled out his gat. "Look, man, she said it's over and I'm only going to say it once. Take your ass on back down the hill where you live." Now, he was in Tyler's face.

Tyler looked at both of them, then down at Rock's gun. Kyra was already halfway down the block. He wanted to call her but he knew she wouldn't even come. So he just turned around and headed down the hill. The people who had gathered, hoping to see some action, were disappointed. Nothing like a rumble in the hood on a nice, sunny day. Tyler vowed to himself, *I'ma get both of them niggas. They don't know who they fucking with.*

When Kyra got back to her house she was still mad. She couldn't believe Tyler tried to play her like that in front of all them people. That fool was trippin'. It only made her madder that it was almost 3:00 and Marvin still hadn't shown up. She thought about walking to his house but decided that would look too desperate. She wasn't going out like that. So she decided to fix a sandwich and something to drink and sit on the porch.

She lived on Hoffman Avenue, the part off of Stuyvesant Avenue. It was a one-way street that had a basketball court. It was the strip. Everyone cruised down Hoffman Avenue with their music pumpin', windows and tops down, smoking weed, drinking and just chillin'. Everybody looking for something to do. She had been sitting on the porch for almost an hour when she noticed the black Mustang convertible easing down the street. Her heart started beating faster. It was him. She tried to act nonchalant when he slowed down in front of her house, holding up the traffic behind him.

"Come here, baby girl," he called. She got up, switching her little hot ass down the steps and went to his car. Her arms were folded. He saw that she was attitude down.

"Damn, baby girl, you look hot in that dress. It's short as hell! You got on panties underneath?"

Kyra's cheeks turned red as fire. "Of course I got on panties!"

"Well, go take 'em off and come get in the car."

Kyra's cheeks turned even redder. "What? Now?"

"You heard me. And hurry up. I'm holding up traffic."

She looked at him to see if he was going to crack a smile. He was dead serious. She ran in the house, snatched off the panties, ran back out and jumped in his car. Marvin pulled off, heading straight for his apartment. He looked at Kyra and grinned. He was getting hard just thinking about what he was getting ready to do. He wanted to hit it while she had on that little tennis dress. That thought made his dick even harder. He couldn't wait. As soon as they walked into the apartment building he told her to come under the stairwell where the mailboxes were. He pulled her close and started kissing and sucking on her lips. When she felt how hard his dick was, she started smiling.

"Why are you smiling?" he asked her while he was rubbing on her butt.

"I'm smiling because I didn't think you missed me this much. As long as it took for you to pick me up, I was beginning to think that you wasn't coming."

"You thought I wasn't coming to get all this, as good as this is? What about you? Did you miss me?"

"Of course I missed you." And she bit his lip.

"Ooh, I like that," Marvin said. "What else you got for me?" He started rubbing the inside of her thighs. She unbuckled his belt and unzipped his pants. He slipped two fingers inside her pussy and moved them around just the way she liked. When she started moaning and groaning, he lifted her up onto the crate that was against the wall. Kyra grabbed his dick and put it inside her. He grabbed onto her butt and started humping and grinding. His dick was so deep inside her that it only took a few minutes before Kyra was coming. Marvin was caught without a condom again, so he couldn't release himself. After her body stopped trembling and she was relaxed, they stood and kissed passionately.

"How long are you going to be my baby girl?" he asked her, looking into her eyes.

"How long are you going to want me to?"

"Forever," he said. "Regardless of what happens."

"How long are you going to be my man?"

"How long would you want me to be your man?"

"Forever," she said.

"Let's go upstairs so that we can finish this off right."

Chapter 16

Kyra was sprung, and so was Marvin. He left all of his other girlfriends alone. He had to reserve all of his energy for Kyra. She would not let him go a day without dicking her down. His other girlfriends were mad that they got kicked out the picture by a 14-year-old, but Kyra didn't care. Marvin gave her everything she wanted.

In a little over a year, Kyra and Marvin both were strung out on heroin. They went from snorting it, to skin popping to straight shooting up. Kyra quit school and her mother kicked her out. She moved in with Marvin. She no longer stayed in touch with Angel, Roz, or Jaz. Her world was heroin and Marvin. His business was still going strong, if not stronger. He just got hooked on his own product. They both would have been goners if the following string of events didn't happen.

Marvin had set up a meeting with his new contact to buy 20 kilos of heroin. They were supposed to meet at the Round. Marvin had Kyra, Rock, and Snail with him. The sellers were from Connecticut. Two dudes, Shaheim and Twist. Twist was Snail's cousin, so that put Marvin at ease enough to let his baby girl hang out with them.

When they got to the Round, Marvin scanned the parking lot for any unusual activity. He didn't see any undercovers or would-be jackets, but he did see a Ford Bronco with Connecticut tags.

"Yo! There's my cousin's ride," hollered Snail.

"Good," said Marvin. He had one hand on the steering wheel and the other on Kyra's thigh. He parked his car on the side and checked out the parking lot. Everything looked okay so far. Nothing out of the ordinary. Unfortunately, he didn't notice anything suspicious about the gray Ford minivan parked in the back with Tyler, Mark, Cochise, and Tone all crouched down, waiting for them to pass by. All four of them were strapped and ready to handle their business.

Ty had been waiting too long to get his revenge on Marvin. Even after all this time, he still couldn't get over the fact that this fuckin' junkie drug dealer had stolen his girl. When his boy Mark told him that he'd seen Marvin and Kyra a few times at the Round, Ty started forming a plan. He'd been watching them for months, having his boys follow them. Once he figured out that the Round was where Marvin did most of his business, he knew it was only a matter of time before he could get him in the parking lot. Ty and his boys had been parking there for the past four nights, waiting for Marvin to show. Tonight was the night his plan would go into action, and judging from the briefcase Marvin was carrying, Ty thought they might even get away with a little loot when everything was said and done.

"Y'all just make sure Kyra don't get hurt," he reminded his boys.

"Yeah, whatever, Ty. Just chill," said Mark as he sat back to wait until everything would go down.

When Marvin and his crew stepped into the restaurant, they found Twist and Shaheim, already seated and eating up everything. Twist looked up with a mouth full of fries.

"What up, dawg?" he said to his cousin as he stood up, grabbed his napkin and wiped his mouth. "Come sit down. You'll have to excuse us. We was hungry as hell!" Twist was about 6 feet 4 inches and skinny as a rail. He looked like a bean pole wearing a designer suit.

After everybody got seated, was introduced and had ordered, the negotiating started.

"Yo, man. First let me say what a fine young sister you got with you tonight," Twist told Marvin as he looked at Kyra. Kyra smiled like she knew she was the bomb. She had on a tan Chanel, two-piece, short-sleeve pantsuit with hip hugging pants and a double chain, wrapped belt. She had on tan Valentino ankle strap sandals and her nails were manicured, her feet neatly pedicured. She visited the hairdresser twice a week to keep her short bob looking good. Even though they were both junkies, Marvin made sure that they didn't look like it.

"Yeah, my girl's all that," Marvin answered. "But we ain't here to talk about her. Let's get down to business." He may have stayed high most of the time, but Marvin still was sharp as a tack when it came to buying and selling dope.

"Of course y'all understand that I want to try your product before I give up any loot," he told Twist and Shaheim.

"No problem," Shaheim answered as Twist slid two small bags across the table. "That there is straight from the main stash."

Kyra was squirming in her seat because she couldn't wait to get her hands on some of that dope. Marvin handed her a bag. She kissed him on the cheek.

"I'll be right back, baby," she said. "I gotta go to the car for my cosmetics bag."

"Why? You look fine, baby girl," Marvin told her.

"I have to get my works," she whispered into his ear as she got up from the table. As she left to go to the car, Marvin was right behind her, headed to the men's room with his little bag of dope.

Tyler and his boys were still outside in the van, watching the door of the restaurant. When Tyler saw Kyra come out, his heart went to pounding and his chest felt heavy. He was still in love with her. He'd never gotten over the fact that she just walked out of his life without any explanation. He hadn't even had a serious girlfriend in the year and a half since Kyra left him. They watched in silence as Kyra shuffled around in the front of Marvin's car, then went back to the restaurant looking agitated.

"Damn, Ty!" Cochise hollered after she went back inside. "I see why you going all out to get that back. She look like she taste good!"

"Hell, yeah. She's all that," Tone agreed.

"Ty wasn't hittin' it deep enough." Mark was joking. He didn't know how close to the truth he was.

Ty ignored his boys. He was too busy thinking about Kyra. Seeing her brought back a lot of old feelings. *It's just something about her that turns a nigga all the way out*, he thought. He wanted her back, and he knew what he would have to do to get her. That's what he was doing in the parking lot with his boys, and now he was anxious to get this shit over with.

"Them niggas will be out shortly. Don't fuck up!" he warned them.

"We straight!" yelled Cochise.

"Yeah, we got this," said Tone. He was agitated because Ty kept going over the fucking plan with them. Mark was sitting in the back, pulling on a blunt. He just nodded his head.

Everyone was silent as Ty started the engine and slowly drove the van around front. He left the engine running and they all put on their ski masks and waited.

Back in the restaurant, Snail and Rock were still sitting at the table with the dudes from Connecticut, waiting for Marvin to get back.

"Damn, that must be some good shit. That nigga ain't back yet," Snail joked.

"My shit is always Grade A. That's the only way to keep the East Coast on lock," Shaheim boasted.

"Where's Marvin?" Kyra came back to the table looking mad.

"He still in the bathroom, baby girl," Rock told her. "Why don't you have a seat till he come back?"

Kyra was pacing nervously, and everyone at the table knew what her problem was.

"Yo, Kyra," Twist grabbed her arm. "You a'ight? Anything we can do to help you, baby girl?"

"Not unless you got my cosmetics bag with you," she snarled at him, rubbing her hands up and down her arms. "I thought that shit was in the car, but it ain't there."

"Can't help you there," said Rock. He hated to see Kyra so strung out, but he could never say anything to Marvin about it unless he wanted to get his ass kicked.

Kyra waited, pacing the whole time, for what felt like hours. Really, it was only five minutes, but she couldn't take it anymore.

"Damn!" she muttered. "Tell Marvin I'll meet him back at the house. I gotta go get something." Without waiting for an answer, she went outside and walked to the cab stand down the block. She couldn't wait to get home and get some of the "H" into her veins.

From the parking lot, Ty could see her rushing to a cab and he was relieved. He didn't know why she was leaving, but he was glad Kyra wouldn't be around when the bullets started flying. Later tonight he'd go find her where she stayed with Marvin and take her back to his place. Then they could start over.

Twist was getting impatient inside the restaurant. Marvin was taking way too long in the bathroom.

"Let me go check on a nigga. We need to be wrapping this

shit up," he told everyone else at the table. He went to pay the bill and then go find Marvin.

"Excuse me, miss," he said as he approached the hostess and pulled out his wallet. "Do you take Visa Platinum?"

She looked down at his wallet and gave him a big smile, her gold tooth glittering. He took that as an invitation.

"What time do you get off tonight, Latifah?" he asked, reading her name tag.

"You don't want none of this!" she told him as she took his credit card.

"How do you know what I don't want?" he asked her. She handed him back his card and a receipt to sign.

"Trust me," she said.

"Why don't you come with me in the bathroom?"

"Fuck you!" she spat.

"Oh, you is a feisty ho, huh?" He grabbed his dick.

Latifah gave him the finger and walked away. Twist shrugged and grabbed some peppermints out of the glass bowl on the counter. He headed for the restroom. As soon as he opened the door, the smell of old air freshener hit him in the face. He didn't step inside, just stuck his head in and yelled for Marvin.

"Yo, man, you a'ight? We waitin' on you!"

"Yeah. Here I come, man." Marvin's slurred voice bounced off the walls. "Where's Kyra?"

"She said to tell you meet her back at the house. Somethin' about her cosmetics bag," Twist hollered and closed the bathroom door.

Marvin finally got back to the table. He gave Rock a nod, and Rock gave Shaheim the briefcase with the cash in it. Shaheim opened it up, went through it, and slammed it shut. He nodded at his partner.

"Why don't y'all bring your car around so we can do this

transaction?" Twist said. Everyone got up from the table and headed outside. Snail went to get Marvin's car, and Marvin and Rock went with Twist and Shaheim to their Bronco. Ty saw them head to the car with the Connecticut plates and he started inching his way closer until he was right next to the Bronco.

"Yo, it's on!" Tone sounded like he couldn't wait to start shooting.

As soon as Twist unlocked the Bronco and opened the trunk, Ty and his boys threw open the doors to the van. Marvin, Twist, Shaheim and Rock turned to see 3 tech-9s and a Desert Eagle staring them in the face. Rock went for his gun, but Ty wasted no time putting a couple through his chest. Rock's body jerked up and down and then hit the ground. For a second, everyone froze except for Tone. He dragged Rock's limp body to the back of the Bronco. Ty grabbed the briefcase with the cash and threw it in the van.

"Get in the fuckin' car!" he yelled at Marvin, Twist and Shaheim. None of them moved as they watched Mark and Cochise in wide-eyed horror. They were unloading the dope from the Bronco and throwing it into the back of the van. As high as he was, Marvin was feeling weak. He was watching twenty kilos of dope and all his fuckin' cash being taken right before his eyes. Not to mention Rock's blood was spattered all over his designer clothes.

Snail pulled Marvin's car around from the back and saw what was going down. He saw Rock's bloody body sprawled on the ground and knew it was too late to do anything. He just kept right on driving, leaving tire tracks as he sped out of the parking lot.

Tyler forced Twist and Shaheim into the front seats, and then ordered Marvin to put Rock's body in the trunk of the Bronco. Marvin cringed, but he couldn't leave his boy there. He would put the body in the car and deal with these punk-ass niggas another time. He figured that once he put the word out, these dudes would be dead anyway. He lifted Rock into the Bronco and turned to face Ty. He was gonna warn him to watch his back, 'cause this shit was definitely not over.

Ty didn't give him time to say anything. "This is for taking what's mine, nigga!" Ty lifted the mask off his face so his face would be the last thing Marvin saw before he died. He shot Marvin three times in the chest. Marvin's body fell back against the open trunk of the Bronco, and Ty shoved it the rest of the way in, slamming the door.

"Now take your asses back to Connecticut and don't ever fucking come back!" Ty told Shaheim.

"What the fuck am I supposed to do with two bodies?"

"Look, nigga I ain't got no beef with you. You can either join them or take 'em with you. What's it gonna be, partna?" Tyler asked, cocking his piece. Shaheim started up the Bronco and pulled off. The whole thing had taken less than ten minutes to go down.

Tyler and his crew jumped in the van, took off their ski masks and put away the guns. They took off out of the Round parking lot, whooping and hollering about all the loot and dope they'd just scored.

"Damn, Ty! That shit was off the hook. We got mad loot off them fools." Mark laughed from the backseat.

"Yo, did you see that punk-ass Marvin before you shot him? Nigga looked so stoned he couldn't hardly see straight!" Cochise joined in the laughter. Tone was opening the briefcase to start counting the money.

Ty looked in the rearview mirror at his boys and shook his head. Yeah, he was happy about the way things went down, but it wasn't the money or the dope that he was interested in at the moment.

"Yo. I got to find Kyra before she hears what happened," Ty said.

"That's cool, man," said Tone. "But don't sweat it. Ain't like no one could tell her who did her man. The only eyewitnesses are taking their punk asses back to Connecticut as we speak. All you gots to do is swoop in and hold Kyra while she boo-hoos about her man. I guarantee you will get some of that pussy before the week is over."

Ty drove the van back to Tone's crib, where he dropped off Tone and Mark. He told them to sit tight and stash the loot until he and Cochise came back. He just had to make sure Kyra was straight, then they'd figure out how to start moving this dope on the streets.

Cochise and Ty dumped the stolen van in a deserted alley and then went to get Ty's car. Ty knew where Marvin and Kyra were staying because he'd been following them for a few weeks, so that was the first place they went to look for her. He was relieved when he pulled up and saw all the lights were on. She was probably in there wondering why Marvin hadn't brought his sorry ass home yet. Ty would be the one to break the sad news to her. He could play like his boys had seen it all go down and then he rushed over there to check on her as soon as he heard about it. She'd never figure out he had something to do with Marvin's death. He could worry about the rest of the details later. Right now he just couldn't wait to get in there and see Kyra.

Cochise waited in the car while Ty ran up to the front door and started banging. He could hear the music playing inside, but no one came to the door. He banged again, calling Kyra's name. When he still didn't get an answer, he peeked through the front window, and that's when he saw her.

"Oh, shit! No!" he screamed. Cochise heard him and came running just as Ty slammed his body against the door and broke the lock. The door swung in and slammed against the wall. They looked down and saw Kyra, lying on the floor with a needle stuck in her arm and white foam oozing out the sides of her mouth.

"Fuck! Fuck! Fuck!" hissed Tyler as he bent down to feel her neck. He was relieved that she still had a faint pulse.

"Go get me a glass of salt water and a bucket of ice," he ordered Cochise. "And call 911."

Tyler's brother Bone had been a heroin addict for years, so he knew exactly what to do. It made him sick to his stomach whenever his brother OD'd. Sometimes, instead of trying to save him he was tempted to let him die. This time, there was no way he was gonna let Kyra die.

Cochise came back with the salt water and ice. "Get the fuck outta here before 5-0 shows. I'll handle this," Tyler told his boy. Cochise bolted out the door.

Tyler removed the syringe that was hanging out of Kyra's arm. She looked like a ghost lying there on the floor. A ghost dressed in designer clothes. He couldn't believe she had sunk this low. A junkie. He squirted out the little bit of dope in the syringe and then filled it with salt water. He was glad that he could easily find a vein on her small arms. As soon as a vein popped up he pumped in the solution.

"Come on, Kyra!" He smacked her and gave her mouth-to-mouth. He put the ice cubes around her neck and on her chest.

"Come on, baby. Stay with me," he kept repeating until the paramedics finally arrived.

Chapter 17

When Kyra woke up in the hospital, she didn't remember anything after the moment she put the needle in her veins. All she knew was she felt like shit and wasn't quite sure where she was. She struggled to focus her eyes and look around the room. That's when she saw Ty, asleep in a chair by her bed. He hadn't left her side the entire time she was in that hospital.

"Ty?" Kyra said in a weak voice. "Is that you? Where the fuck am I?"

Ty stirred from his sleep when he heard her voice. He smiled at her. It didn't matter to him how sick she still looked. He was just so happy she had pulled through.

"Hey, girl. I been waiting to hear that voice ever since they brought you in here."

"Where? Tell me where I am, Ty." Kyra was so confused.

"You're at the hospital, Kyra."

"Why am I here? Who brought me here?" She tried to sit up in the bed, but was too weak.

"You came in an ambulance. I found you OD'd on your floor. You almost died from that shit, you know." Ty shuddered at the memory.

"How long I been here?" Kyra asked.

"Two days." Kyra turned her head away from Ty and closed her eyes for a second. She was trying to remember what had happened to make her so sick. Finally it came back to her. She remembered being at the Round with Marvin when they got the "H" from Twist and Shaheim. Damn! Why had she left the restaurant without Marvin? He was probably so fuckin' mad that she had OD'd. He was always tellin' her to go easy on that shit, 'cause he didn't need everyone knowing that him and his girl were using the product. But Ty had said he found her on her floor. At least it didn't happen in the restaurant. Maybe word wasn't out on the street. She turned to face Ty again.

"Where's Marvin?" she asked. "I know that nigga must be ready to kick my ass right about now." She tried to laugh, but it took more energy than she had.

Ty shifted in his seat before he answered. While he'd waited for Kyra to wake up, he'd been thinking of the best lie to tell her. First, he wanted to tell her Marvin had left town with some other bitch, but he knew Kyra wouldn't believe that. Then he found out that Marvin's boy Snail had already got the word out on the street about what he saw when he drove away in Marvin's car that night. Nobody had heard from Twist or Shaheim once they headed back to Connecticut with the bodies, but Snail was tellin' everyone he knew that he would pay big for anyone who gave up the four niggas in ski masks who killed Rock. Everyone in the hood knew that Marvin was missing. It was only a matter of time before someone told Kyra the truth. Ty decided he would be the one to tell her. The only detail he left out was how he was the one who pulled the trigger on that motherfucker.

"You ain't got to worry about that nigga Marvin kicking your ass, Kyra."

"What do you mean?" she asked. "He ain't mad that I OD'd?"

"I doubt it," Ty said. "I doubt he's feelin' much of anything right about now." He almost wanted to smile as he thought about how he blew Marvin away.

"Ty, what are you sayin'?" Kyra was starting to get nervous. She felt like she was gonna throw up 'cause she had an idea what Ty was trying to tell her.

Ty told her the story of what happened that night. Of course, he pretended he'd heard it on the street from one of his boys who was at the Round and watched everything go down from inside. He said that his boy saw Marvin take a few bullets before they stuffed his body in the trunk. As far as anyone on the street knew, Marvin and Rock were both dead, their bodies in some car from Connecticut.

Kyra let out a scream and a nurse came running in the room. She kicked Ty out while she calmed Kyra down. When he was finally allowed back into the room Kyra was sedated, but she was still awake.

"So how'd you find me?" she asked Ty in a drowsy voice. "I ain't seen you for over a year, and you happen to show up at my door on the same night Marvin gets shot?"

"Kyra," he said calmly. She was suspicious, but he was ready for her with another lie. "Me and my boys was hangin' that night when we heard what happened. I knew you was gonna be upset since Marvin was your man and all, so I wanted to find you to make sure you didn't do nothin' stupid."

"Yeah?" She almost looked like she wanted to smile at him. Like she knew she'd be dead if Ty hadn't come looking for her. "How'd you know where we lived?"

"Please, girl. Everyone know where Marvin live," Ty answered. Kyra believed him. It wouldn't be that hard for someone to find out where Marvin stayed at. Everyone in the hood knew Marvin.

"I feel like shit," Kyra said. "I need to go to sleep." Without another word, she turned away from Ty and closed her eyes. She was asleep in under a minute and she slept until the next morning.

Ty stayed with Kyra until she was released from the hospital, and he visited her every day for four and a half months while she went through rehab in Princeton. When he wasn't visiting her, he was selling dope. He flipped those twenty kilos they had jacked from Marvin and he eventually ended up being the third largest drug dealer on the East Coast.

Once Kyra accepted that Marvin was dead, she got back with Tyler. She moved in with him after she was released from rehab and got her life back together. She was determined to stay off drugs and leave her past behind her, so she never asked another question about what happened that night at the Round. She got back with her girls, Jaz and Roz and Angel, and they helped her get on the right track. Kyra went back to school, and then on to college.

Things with her and Ty were OK. She still had feelings for him, but they would never be as strong as what she felt for Marvin. Of course, when she got back with Ty, she didn't know that Marvin was actually still alive.

When Shaheim and Twist left the Round, they dumped Rock and Marvin at the hospital and jetted back to Connecticut. Miraculously, Marvin survived his gunshot wounds and spent a month in the hospital. Because of the way he'd been dumped at the hospital with Rock's dead body, the police were called in to investigate. He almost got charged with Rock's murder, and he did get busted on some old charges in New York. After he was released from the hospital, they sent his ass to Sing Sing for seven years. Nobody back in Trenton knew Marvin was even alive until he finally sent a letter to one of his boys. He wanted someone to get word to Kyra that he was getting out in a year, and he was coming back to her. But by the time Kyra heard about it, it was too late. Not only had she moved on with her life, she was getting ready to become a doctor and was thinking about breaking up with Ty. She was through with these thugs from the street.

It took Kyra nearly a year to get up the nerve to break it off with Ty. After all, he'd saved her from getting raped when they were kids, and then he'd saved her life. He'd had her back all these years, and made sure she didn't want for nothin'. But now she was ready. So, here she was, parked in front of Ahmads, Tyler's brother's house, getting ready to face Ty.

Kyra saw Tyler's red Beamer parked on the side of the house as if he were hiding from someone. *I knew he'd be here*, she said to herself. Tyler was always hanging out with his boys, doin' nothing. That was one of the things about him that was driving her crazy. She was working her ass off to become a doctor and he was sitting on his ass most of the time. She grabbed her purse and jumped out the Jeep that Tyler bought for her and put in her name. She rang the doorbell. No one answered, so after a few seconds she rang again. She knew they were in there, but still no one came to the door. Kyra took out her cell phone and dialed. After the first ring, Ahmad answered.

"What's up?"

"Come open the front door!"

"You at the front door?"

"No, Ahmad. I'm at the freakin' back door," Kyra said sarcastically.

"Oh, snap, yo! Ty go answer the door. It's for you."

Tyler came to the front door looking very surprised. He had on no shirt, revealing the six-pack that he sported. He had on baggy Phat Farm jeans and white sweat socks. He looked tired and his eyes were red.

"Hey, baby!" he said as he grabbed Kyra, picked her up and kissed her. "Why'd you drive way up here?"

"We need to talk, Tyler, and it can't wait." Kyra squirmed out of his arms, then folded her arms and stared at him.

She called me Tyler instead of Ty. It must be PMS time, he thought. He ran his fingers across the small mound of hair that grew under his chin and looked at her.

"It's that important that it couldn't wait until I got home?"

"You haven't been home in four days," she reminded him. "I'm moving out this weekend. Half my stuff is already packed."

"What you talking about, moving? Moving where?"

"Out, Tyler. It's over. I need some time to myself. Gotta get myself together."

"What I do?" He stretched out his arms and hunched his shoulders.

Just then, this tall, dark, pretty sister came down the stairwell. She looked at Tyler, then at Kyra.

"I'm Jalisa," she said in a preppy little voice. She held out her hand for Kyra to shake it. Kyra just looked down at Jalisa's fake-ass nails. Jalisa pulled her hand back and rolled her eyes. Tyler just stood there yanking at the mound of hair under his chin. Jalisa turned and looked at Tyler with a seductive smile. "How long are you gonna be in town, Ty?"

Tyler didn't take his eyes off Kyra as he answered. "It depends on this woman here." Jalisa mumbled something no one understood and waltzed out the front door.

"Kyra, why you trippin'?"

"I'm going to use the bathroom and then I'm outta here." Kyra walked to the stairwell.

Tyler wondered what she was trippin' about. It was hard to

read her because she was acting all serious and not saying much. Tyler's pager vibrated as Kyra came down the stairs. He turned it off without even looking at it. Nothing mattered right now but Kyra. She stormed past him, heading for the front door.

"Can I ride with you?" he pleaded.

"Ride in your own car. I need time to clear my mind."

"Wait, Kyra!" As he yelled, he grabbed his Timberlands off the stairs and snatched his shirt from the banister. He ran out the door, trying to keep up with her.

When they got on the front porch, Tyler's baby brother, Lil' Anthony, pulled up and beeped his horn. He was in a cream colored Porsche with chrome rims.

"Where you steal that from?" Ty yelled. Anthony gave Ty the finger and focused on Kyra.

"Hey, Kyra, you want a ride?"

"No, that's all right," she answered. "You need to be careful. I've been worried about you."

"I'm straight, sis-in-law. I'll be down to see you this weekend." He stuck his middle finger up at Ty again and zoomed off.

"That boy is going to get himself killed. You need to talk to him," Kyra told Ty.

"You know nobody can't tell him nothing." Ty wasn't interested in his pain-in-the-ass brother right now. He was still trying to figure out what was up with Kyra, who was opening the door to her Jeep.

"Can I ride with you?" He tried one more time. "I'm tired and ain't been to sleep in two days."

"Tell that shit to Jalisa!" she snapped as she revved the engine.

"Fuck Jalisa!"

"Isn't that what you've been doing for the last four nights?" Kyra backed out the driveway and headed down the street. Tyler ran and got into his Beamer, following close behind her.

On the way home, they stopped once to fill up their tanks. While the attendant was pumping the gas, Tyler begged and pleaded with Kyra to tell him why she wanted to move out. He wasn't about to let her leave him again without an explanation the way she'd done when she got with Marvin.

"C'mon, Kyra. You know we can work this out," he begged.

"Look, Ty." She sighed. "I don't know what else to say to you. This is it. This is the end. We can't go no further."

Ty still followed her all the way back to the apartment, hoping she'd change her mind.

When they walked into the apartment, the alarm sounded, magnifying the headache Kyra already had. She pushed the appropriate buttons to disarm it, then threw her keys on top of the big screen and headed straight for the bathroom. She ran some hot water and poured in some Calgon bath beads. She wanted to be taken away. Tyler was still following her all around asking her why she was trippin'. She tried to explain to him that she couldn't be a doctor living with a drug dealer. It was time for them to move on. The fire was out. He was getting madder when he saw how much of her shit was packed. It was starting to look like she wasn't going to change her mind.

"I know why you trippin'," he finally said as he watched her get in the tub. "I know that nigga Marvin is out."

"This ain't got nothing to do with Marvin. I haven't been fucking him for the last seven years. I've been with you. This is between me and you. There is nothing here no more. Nothing. Can you close the door on your way out, please?" He just stood there looking at her for a few seconds. Then he started pleading. "Don't leave me, Kyra. You know I love you and will do anything for you."

"Can you close the door behind you, please?" she repeated.

He slammed the door, almost shaking the pictures off the wall.

Just as Kyra laid her head back to relax in the tub, the door swung open again.

"You know I ain't going out like this," he snarled at her. "That'll be fucked up if you get back with that nigga." He left, not bothering to close the bathroom door.

Kyra just wanted to relax. She was not gonna let Ty get to her. She had made her decision, and she was gonna stick to it. She got out of the tub, closed the bathroom door and popped four Tylenol, then she got back in the tub and dozed off. When she woke up, the tub water was ice cold and her fingertips and toes were shriveled. It was 2:18 A.M.

She went into the bedroom. Tyler was out cold, snoring. He was making up for the two days he claimed he hadn't slept. As Kyra lotioned up her skin, she heard a knock at the front door. *What the fuck?* She snatched her short satin robe off the back of the door. She figured it was Jaz and Roz. They were the only ones who didn't care what time they called or what time they barged into someone's house. Kyra slid the cover off the peephole and then slammed it back. Her breathing came in rapid, short breaths. She felt like she was hyperventilating. Her back pressed into the door as she slid down and sat her naked butt on the floor.

"Dayum! Dayum! Dayum!" she said out loud.

Marvin was at the door. It had been seven years, but she recognized his face instantly. He was bold as hell, coming here this time of night, knowing that she lived with Tyler.

Knock! Knock! Knock!

She couldn't move. He knocked harder. That got her up, 'cause she didn't want to wake Tyler. She cracked the door as far as the chain would go.

"What's up, baby girl?" he said in that smooth, sweet voice that she remembered so well.

"Do you know what time it is?"

117

"Yeah, I know. But that ain't important. Only thing important is me seein' my baby girl."

"You should have called first and saved yourself a trip."

"I'ma let that remark go."

"Marvin, I have a man in the bedroom, asleep. This is his place."

"Baby girl, I just need five minutes."

"I'm not dressed."

Kyra looked at him and then looked back at the bedroom. Her head was spinning.

"Please. Just five minutes."

Kyra closed the door, slid off the chain and let him in. Her heart felt like it was beating ninety miles an hour, and she could barely breathe. Marvin was looking damned good. He'd put on weight, but it looked like all muscle. He'd grown a fine, thin beard. His head was almost bald. He wore a black Sean Jean denim outfit and the shirt was open, showing off his six-pack. He was wearing Cool Water cologne. The brother was on.

Kyra's head was no longer spinning. Her body was now trembling. Just like it used to whenever he was in her presence. *Prison does a nigga good*, she thought.

Marvin looked her up and down. His heart and his dick were twitching. She looked more mature and her hair was different. She put on a few pounds, but they were definitely in the right places. Other than that, she looked the same as she did seven years ago. She wore a gold colored short, satin robe that exposed those pretty brown legs she used to wrap around his back. He had waited seven years to see his beautiful baby girl again. Marvin felt like he was dreaming.

"The clock is ticking." She was afraid to make eye contact.

Marvin cleared his throat. "Kyra, all I did was think about you and dream about you while I was away. I still love you. I told you that you would be my baby girl forever and I meant it. You told me that you wanted me to be your man forever. I want back in. I want to be your man and take care of you."

"I don't need nobody to take care of me, and you have one minute left."

"Let me be your man like I promised." He was looking her up and down. He could hardly contain himself.

"I got a man, Marvin. You know that."

"Then why are you trembling? And why can't you look at me?" He looked around the room. "Why are these boxes packed? If you care about your man so much, why you movin'?"

"How you know the boxes are mine?"

"I know you, baby girl, and I know you ain't happy."

"I know you don't think you can just walk in here and start where we left off. It's been seven years. People change. I've changed. You've changed. We all change."

"Change is good. We both changed for the better. My love for you has grown, and look at you. Still trembling like you used to."

"Your five minutes is up, Marvin." Kyra opened the door.

"Okay, but just answer me this. Do you still have feelings for me?"

"It's been seven years."

"Do you still have feelings for me? Yes or no? Say no and I'm out." Marvin was really going for it. *I'm almost on my hands and knees begging,* he thought.

Kyra looked at him. She wanted to say no just because she was angry at him. No words would come out. It was something about him standing there in front of her that brought back all those old feelings. She felt the tears welling up. *Oh, shit!* That was the last thing she wanted him to see her do. But it was too late. The tears were coming down. He reached over, grabbed her face and kissed her tears. He took her in his strong arms and held her tight. Kyra was sobbing big time.

"I thought you were dead, Marvin. You were supposed to protect me." She sobbed. "Then, you weren't even there for me when I almost died."

"I'm here for you now, baby girl." He put his lips to hers and tasted her salty tears. "Are you still my baby girl?" he asked her while he wiped her tears away. She looked him in his eyes but she didn't answer. He kissed her again.

"I am so mad at you, Marvin."

"You should be. You don't know how bad I felt. I am so sorry. I'll make it up to you if you let me."

Kyra felt confused as hell. On one hand, here was a nigga who she was crazy about. But he got her strung out on dope, then left her for seven years. Then there was another nigga, sleep in the bed just a few feet away. He'd been there for her since day one, taking care of her and looking out for her. She pushed Marvin back.

"I need some time to sort some things out."

He pulled her close and put his tongue deep in her mouth. She tasted so good. He wasn't planning on letting her go tonight or any other night. He eased his hand down, and in one smooth move he opened her robe. They kept kissing, enjoying the taste of each other. Kyra, just as smooth, tied the robe back. He eased his hand back down and felt between her legs. It was so moist. He slid two fingers across her clit and then slid them inside her. She moaned and grabbed him tighter. He pulled out his fingers and ran his tongue up and down them.

"You still taste so sweet, baby girl. I've been waitin' for this for so long." He kissed her again, opened her robe and stroked her nipples.

"Marvin, we can't do this. He's right in there," she whispered, pushing him away.

"Yes, we can." He pulled her close and kissed her long and hard.

He picked her up, carried her into the kitchen and set her on the counter. He put his mouth on her breasts and licked them like they were ice cream cones. Kyra was on fire. She unbuckled his pants and started stroking him. He was already hard. She guided the head and started rubbing it all over her wet mound. Her moaning got louder and louder. He still remembered what each moan meant. He slid it in, going in as deep as he could.

"Don't move," she said. It was in so deep and Kyra just wanted to savor the feeling that only he could give her. Marvin always felt so good. He always took his time and made sure she was satisfied. She kissed him and told him how much she'd missed him. Then she told him to make her come real hard. Marvin humped so hard that each time he came out and went back in he lifted her off the counter. Kyra wrapped her legs around his back and held on for dear life.

"Marvin! Marvin! Marv—" she moaned as her body went limp. He went back to licking her nipples, neck, ears, and then sucking on her tongue. His dick was still in deep and it was still hard.

"You okay, baby girl?"

She looked him in the eyes and kissed him softly on his lips. "Damn, I've missed you," she said.

"I know. I've missed you, too."

Kyra started gyrating her hips, making him even harder inside her.

"I ain't got no protection on, baby girl, and I'm gonna come real hard if you don't stop."

She stopped moving. "How much do you miss me?" she whispered.

"More than you'll ever know."

"Kiss me," she said. He did as he eased out of that place where he'd dreamt about being for seven years. Then she put both feet on the counter and slowly pushed his head down between her legs. He parted her lips and began licking and sucking. It was driving her crazy. She moaned and groaned and gyrated those hips until she exploded again. She lay back on the counter as limp as a rag doll. Marvin grabbed some paper towels, wiped himself, her and the counter.

"Go pack the rest of your shit, baby girl. I'm taking you with me." Before she could protest, he said, "I don't want to hear shit about that nigga in the other room, 'cause obviously he ain't handling his business. You act like you ain't been fucked in months."

Kyra looked at him as he lifted her off the counter. He leaned down and kissed her.

"Go ahead. Pack the rest of your shit. I'll start taking the other boxes downstairs."

She did as she was told.

Marvin had taken off his shirt while he was carrying her stuff downstairs. After the last of the stuff was in the truck, he told Kyra to wait in the truck while he went up to get his shirt. When he got into the apartment, he pulled out his gat and went into the bedroom. He pressed the hard steel to Tyler's nose. Ty's eyes popped wide open.

"What's up, partna?" Marvin said to Tyler. "Who got the upper hand now? I know you ain't think I was gonna let you slide with robbin' me and killin' my boy. You dumb motherfucker."

"Fuck you!" Tyler spat, with the steel stuck to his nose.

"If you would have been fucking your woman, she wouldn't

have been packing. I'm enjoying this. This is my day. I just got done fucking her right in your kitchen, man. I can't believe how dumb you are. However, I do appreciate you looking out for her and keeping her safe while I was gone. See you in hell, partna!"

PART THREE

Jaz

Chapter 18

"Taylor! Bag and baggage!" C.O. Johnson coughed as the Camel dangled from her lips.

"Bust the fucking gates!" yelled Micki Taylor, Jaz's twenty-nine-year-old sister.

"Don't come back no time soon. Let us at least get a chance to wash your sheets," C.O. Johnson barked sarcastically.

"Don't worry about me. I'ma be a'ight," Micki said with a nervous squeak in her voice. She picked up the army green duffle bag that held the stuff she'd collected over the last five years. Then she flopped down on the metal bench and stared at the sign that read "Receiving and Discharging—Clinton Correctional Women's Facility."

She let out a long sigh. The correctional facility had been her residence for the last half decade, ever since she was convicted for possession and trafficking crack cocaine. She rubbed her sweaty hands, then got down on her knees and prayed.

"Oh, Lord, please give me the strength to stay on the right path. Thank you for keeping my three daughters, Tameka, Shadai and Misa safe for me. Thank you for allowing them to forgive me

127

and not forget me. I want to be a mother to them and take care of them. Please give me strength. Amen."

"Good-bye, Pink. Take care of yourself." That was her drug counselor, Mr. Rhames. He waved at her and kept on going. They had developed a pretty good friendship during the time Micki was locked up. He always teased her, telling her she looked just like the white punk rocker who went by the name Pink.

"Let's go, Taylor," another officer shouted.

Here goes to be being free, Micki said to herself as the metal gates clicked, clanged, and clacked to slide open and set her free. Then it clicked, clanged, and clacked to keep the rest of the sisters inside.

The sun was shining bright as she stepped outside on this crisp October day. Micki was looking forward to seeing her baby sister, Jaz. She set her green duffle bag on the ground, stretched out her arms, looked up at the sky and yelled, "I'm Freeeee!" as she twirled around in circles. People were passing by on their way to work or to visit relatives who were locked up, but no one paid her any attention. She slowed her circles and leaned over, resting her hands on her knees. That's when she burst out laughing. She felt so good. At least, until she looked up and saw a white man with greasy, slicked back hair. He was blowing kisses in her direction. She stood up and glared at him.

"Well, hello, Mr. Hamilton." Micki smirked, folding her arms. It was her jive-ass public defender.

"Hello." He grinned as he extended his hand. "And you are?"

"Why do you want to know?" His sorry ass didn't even recognize her.

"I was going to offer you a ride. It looks like you need one."

"You don't even recognize me, do you? You slimy mother-fucker!" She spat. His face reddened.

"It's Micki Taylor, Mr. Sign-this-MissTaylor-and-the-most-you'll-do-is-two-years. You greaseball. I ended up doing five fuckin' years thanks to your sorry ass! I hope you burn in hell!" She picked up a handful of rocks and threw them at him. He ran.

Honk! Honk! Honk!

Micki turned at the sound of the car horn. It was a Cadillac Escalade, and a woman was hanging out the window, pointing a video camera.

"Busted!" Angel yelled. "Throwing rocks at a white man! Ain't been out of jail five minutes and already you committing a crime!"

Micki screamed and ran toward the car. Jaz and Roz jumped out of the car. Everyone was screaming, jumping up and down. Angel was walking, holding the video camera steady, trying to tape this Kodak moment.

"Welcome to the free world, big sis." Jaz kissed her eldest sister and grabed her in a big bear hug.

"Dayum! You been killing the potatoes, dawg!" Roz joked.

"Puh-leese! You should have seen my big ass two months ago. I was 160 pounds. Now I'm down to 142." Micki grinned, turning and spinning, trying to walk like a model.

"Come give me a hug, you yellow heifer," Micki joked at Angel.

"It takes one to know one. You lighter than me!" Angel laughed, then said, "Your hair is the shit. They got them kind of skills up in there?"

"Yeah. You got every kind of skill imaginable behind bars. Some of the sisters got it going on. I'ma miss a few of them, but I ain't going back. Let's get the fuck outta here before they change their minds." They all hopped in the Escalade.

"Lil' sis, you gotta be slangin' something to be rocking this shit! This is nice. I wish my homegirls could have seen me jump into this." She opened the glove compartment.

"Faheem bought this for me," Jaz said.

"Oh, yeah. Faheem. I like that picture of you and him that you sent me. That nigga is fine. He look like Method Man, only a little better. I would love to hit that!"

"Don't even think about it, my sister. Ain't no man swapping in this family." They all laughed.

"You got that nigga sprung anyway, from what I heard. See, we get all the gossip that goes on out here in the so-called free world. Them hos up in there be talking about the ballers, and his name comes up quite often. They say he's a freak. They can't wait to get out to get with that. He be slangin' hard I heard. Naw, but I did hear that he done chilled as far as the hos are concerned."

"He used to deal, but not anymore. Them hos can forget it. He's my freak now. I got that on lock."

"I hear you, baby sis. Handle your business."

"How he buy this car?"

"He own liquor stores all over town. No matter what side of town you go to. North, south, east or west. He got it on lock."

"Shit, he make that much loot just sellin' liquor?" Micki asked.

"Not exactly," Jaz admitted. "He's sellin' counterfeit bills."

"Yeah," added Roz. "And the shits look real, girl."

"That's right. My man be pullin' in money by the truckload in his business," Jaz said proudly.

"Dayum! That's what I'm talking bout. Don't fuck it up, Jaz. Take it from me. I got three babies and three babies' daddies. Only one of them is worth something. When you find some man who'll take care of you and love you, you better hold on to him. And it's bonus if he can fuck you. You hear me?"

"I hear you."

"Why was you throwing rocks at that white dude?" Angel asked.

"That was my fucking shithead public defender. I hate him. I'm glad I wasn't packing a gat," hissed Micki.

"I'm glad, too," Roz said. "You ain't bringing me down for conspiracy to murder."

"I feel you. Where's your cousin Kyra?" Micki asked, turning around to look at Angel.

"That's a long story," Angel said.

"Well, start talking. We got a two and a half hour drive, and I want to know all the gossip."

"I thought you hear everything on the inside," teased Angel.

"I want to hear it from the horse's mouth. Not the watered down version."

"Well, you know that nigga Marvin got out, right?"

"Hell, yeah. That's another name that comes up all the time. He did seven years at Sing Sing. They say he look finer than before he went upstate. And they say he is paid."

"Anyway, the same day he got out he went to see Kyra, and the bitch was living in Tyler's crib. Tyler was asleep and Marvin fucked her right there in Tyler's house. Then he made Kyra pack her shit and he took her with him that same night. He went back and smoked Tyler. Now Marvin and Kyra live somewhere in the boondocks with all these bougie black folks."

"And she five months pregnant!" Jaz put her two cents in.

"What? He went to the nigga's house and fucked her? Dayum. That nigga ain't nothing nice. This sound like some TV Mafia shit. He must have been puttin' it down for her to go back with him after seven fuckin' years," Micki said. "Now that's some gossip! Well, is Kyra happy?"

"Every time we see her she is. He got her a house, and that shit is laid!" Roz said.

"Well, at least somebody's happy. Me? I just wanna stay out of trouble. No more drugs. I just wanna go home and sit in the tub and spend time with my children. I got to get to know them all over again." She got quiet as she stared out the window. "Misa is five and a half years old now. Shadai is seven and Tameka is eight. They don't know me."

"Stop the sentimental shit, Micki. Tonight is girls' night out. I got it all planned. One more day ain't gonna hurt what's already done. You can start playing mommy tomorrow," said Jaz. "Faheem got us a limo. We gonna eat at Sylvia's restaurant in Harlem, then we goin' clubbin'."

"E-yeah, e-yeah! e-yeah! We be clubbin! Everybody like it when a girl shake sumthin'! We be clubbin'!" They all were bouncing, trying to sing Ice Cube's joint. They belted out the tune until none of them knew the rest of the words, then they burst out laughing.

"Serious y'all. Get fly. Put on your hoochie gear and be at my momma's crib at 7:30. The limo will be picking us up from there," Jaz instructed.

Jaz dropped off Roz and then Angel. She and Micki headed for their mother's house. Their dad was waiting on the porch. They had the house decorated inside and out. Micki's daughters were all dressed up, and they each had a gift for her. Grandma Rachel, Micki and Jaz's mom, dad and their two brothers, Punk Eddy and Darien, with his four kids, were all there. Their sister Tanisha and her two kids were there as well. Everyone was glad to see that Micki was home.

Chapter 19

After a little welcome home party with Micki and their family, Jaz put on a beige miniskirt by Bisou Bisou, some brown leather Boudicca boots and a cashmere beige sweater. She left her mother's house to go catch up with Faheem. Because of school and work she hadn't seen him in two days, and she missed him. She drove toward his west side liquor store, hoping to see his Jag parked out front. It was there, so she pulled up behind it, turned off the engine and popped a peppermint Certs in her mouth. She had a smile on her face as she went inside.

"Hey, Uncle John. Buzz me back," she said to Faheem's Uncle John. Uncle John was 6 foot 4 inches, bald, brown-skinned, and wore an eye patch over his right eye. He ran this liquor store on the west side of town for Faheem.

"What's shaking, Miss Jazzy?" He said as he pushed the buzzer.

"I just dropped off Micki. She's home."

"Oh, yeah? That's good. Jack and Glenda are getting too old to be watching all them youngins. I hope she stay out of trouble."

"Me, too. Where's Faheem?"

"That knucklehead is back there in his office."

Faheem's door was locked. Jaz knocked. The radio was blasting "It Wasn't Me" by Shaggy. She knocked louder.

"It's me," she yelled.

The door popped open. Faheem had a blunt hanging out his mouth and a pile of money in his hands. He was counting money, then wrapping it in colored paper strips with dollar signs on them. It was impossible for Jaz to tell which bills were real.

"Hey, baby." She went over and kissed him on the cheek. She took off her brown snakeskin jacket and set it with the matching handbag on the chair across from Faheem. "I just dropped Micki at the house. She can't wait to meet you."

After he finished counting the last stack, he put the blunt down. "She a'ight?"

"She seem like it. Nervous, but she seem okay. She claims that she's gonna stay on the straight and narrow. But we'll see. I hope so, for the kids' sake," Jaz said as she watched Faheem stack the piles of money.

"Why you got that short-ass skirt on?" Faheem said. "Come here." Jaz got up and sat on Faheem's lap. He kissed her, sucking on her tongue to taste the peppermint Certs she'd just swallowed. He started kissing her neck.

"Don't start nothing you ain't gonna finish," she whispered in his ear.

"Baby, you know I takes care of mines," he said. "That's why you came over here wearing this short-ass skirt. You ain't slick. I know what you up to." He started unbuttoning her sweater. Jaz had on no bra. Faheem started biting on her nipples. She couldn't think straight when he did that.

"You think you know me so well. Who else's nipples you been sucking on like this?" she teased while she licked his ear.

"I only like to bite on yours. Yours always taste like choco-

134

late." He reached under her skirt and pulled off her moist thong. She unfastened his jeans and pulled out his dick.

"Where're your condoms?" she asked him as she squeezed it and made it harder.

"You ain't got one?" he asked her through his moans.

"Why should I carry them around with me? I ain't fuckin' nobody else."

"You better not be," he said as he flicked his finger back and forth real fast across her clit.

"Baby, that feels so good," she moaned in his ear. Faheem kissed her deeply as he slid two fingers in and out of her wet tunnel. She held on tight as her hips gyrated round and round.

"Faheem, where is your condom?" she asked, licking the sweat off her top lip.

"I know you ain't try'na say a nigga can't get none of his pussy just 'cause he ain't got no latex?"

"Yes, that's what I'm saying."

"A'ight." He started biting on her nipples again and went back to flicking his fingers over her clit. Jaz's breathing got heavier and she started moaning and groaning. He grabbed his dick and slid it on in. Jaz wrapped her legs around his back and the chair rocked back and forth as Faheem pumped inside her. The deeper he went the louder Jaz hollered. Finally, they both exploded in unison and sat there holding each other.

"Ummm. Thank you, baby," she whispered in his ear. "Don't forget my trip to New York is tonight."

"It's tonight?" He sounded surprised. "I thought it was Saturday."

"Don't try to front, Faheem. You knew we was taking Micki out. You got the limo and VIP passes."

"Shit! I thought it was Saturday. I'm supposed to meet some people there. What time is it?" He looked at the clock on his desk. "I got shit to do." He lifted her off his lap and stood to kiss her one more time. "Don't be in New York getting into no shit, Jaz, or this will be your last time going."

"Listen to you. I'ma act like you didn't even say that," she said as she picked up her thong off the desk. "What you need to be doing is stop trying to get me pregnant. This is the last time you're going to hit it without any latex!"

He buckled up his pants and looked at her. "What's the matter with getting pregnant?" He walked over to her and started caressing her butt.

"You know I want to finish school first."

He started to say something, but kissed her instead, circling his tongue around inside her mouth. She felt him getting hard and stepped back.

"I need to wash up before I go get my hair done." She went into the bathroom, and when she came out he was on the phone. She kissed him and mouthed, *Catch you later.*

Chapter 20

The limo arrived at 7:30 on the dot. The four divas were dressed to impress. Jaz sported a red leather tube top and a black leather miniskirt by Anton, with ruby-studded ankle boots by Cesare Paciotti. Since her hair was naturally curly, she had her hairdresser wash and condition it, and trim it. Angel wore a leopard print jumpsuit that cleaved almost to her belly button and was open all down her back. She'd sprinkled gold dust all over her exposed skin. Micki wore a black mini-dress by Plein Sud and some black leather Gucci shoes. Her hair was short and spiked. Roz wore a python tube top and python pants by Andasimo. She had a fur scarf covering her shoulders. Her hair was in a bob, flipped up. They were definitely in the house.

During the limo ride from Jersey to New York, they reminisced, drank champagne, listened to music and chilled. The only thing missing was their girl Kyra. Micki was so happy to be out that she cried. It felt good to be free. Free as in no jail and no drugs. And it felt good to be accepted by her family.

The first stop was Sylvia's Soul Food spot in Harlem. It was good that they had reservations 'cause the place was packed. Once they were seated, they ordered a feast of fried whiting, curry chicken, macaroni and cheese, brown rice with mixed vegetables, a broccoli casserole, carrot soufflé, gingered asparagus and whole wheat biscuits. After tasting a little of everything, no one had room for dessert. Jaz had them wrap the leftovers so she could take a plate to Faheem and give the other one to the limo driver. It was a little after 11:00 when they left Sylvia's. Time to go clubbin'.

Faheem had gotten them some VIP passes for a party thrown by the New Jersey Nets. The limo brought them to the front of the club, where people were still standing in line, hoping to get in. You could hear the music pumping all the way outside. The girls headed past the fools in line, and went straight to the bouncer. Once they flashed their VIP passes, he lifted the velvet ropes and let them in.

"Welcome, beautiful ladies," he said as he held open the door for them. They stood in the doorway and checked the place out. The joint was jumpin'. Kid Capri was the DJ and of course he was settin' it off.

"This is a nice club." Micki admired the décor and the beautiful people everywhere. "Very nice."

"Ooh, I see Stephon Marbury," Angel said. "I'm taking him home tonight."

Roz said, "We just got here. I have to look around first."

A hostess came over and asked the group to follow her. While they walked to their table, the brothers in the joint were checking them out. By the time they sat down, niggas were already sending drinks to their table, asking them to dance. Every one of them refused to dance because they decided to sit for a few to down their drinks and check out the crowd. Micki was all the way live. She was the first one to step out on the dance floor, dancing with two brothers at one time. Mystical screamed "Shake your ass," and both Angel and Roz had to jump up for that one.

Jaz was hoping Faheem would show, so she just sat at the table, chillin'. That's when she noticed this fine brother checking her out. He looked like Eric Benet, even had the dreads. Shaggy was moaning "Mr. Boombastic." Jaz had to get up for that one. As soon as she did, the Eric Benet look-alike came over and followed her to the dance floor. They were groovin' right through to Ludacris dropping bows. Jaz was getting hot, so she excused herself from Eric and went to freshen up. She squeezed her way to the ladies' room past the ballers, ball players, and rappers. This was the place to be. *Not one scrub in the place.* She smiled to herself.

After she freshened up and managed to get back to her table, the waitress brought over another drink. She told Jaz it was from the fine baller heading her way. Jaz looked up and saw the brother.

"You ain't never lied!" Jaz said to the waitress who walked away with a smile. This brother was Ginuwine F-I-N-E. He had on a light gray, silk Italian suit. Jaz admired it as he came and stood directly in front of her.

"Can I join you?" he asked.

"Sure," Jaz answered with a sexy grin.

"My friends call me Smooth." He extended his hand.

"I'm Jaz. Nice to meet you. And thanks for the drink."

"The pleasure is all mine."

They made small talk for about a half hour. Jaz found out that homeboy played for the New Jersey Nets, as a rookie and had graduated from Princeton two years ago. They had a lot to talk about since that was Jaz's school. He had gotten his B.A. in biochemistry, so Jaz was taking a lot of the classes he had already taken. The conversation was real cool, and he wanted to talk to her again. He gave Jaz all of his numbers. She gave him her pager number. Jay-Z started crooning "HOV! HOV!"

"Wanna dance?" he asked her.

"Let's go!" Jaz bounced out of her seat without hesitation. They danced through Jay-Z rapping "Give It to Me," Q-Tip's "Vivrant Thing," Ruff Endz saying "No More," and Shaggy swearing "It Wasn't Me." When they heard Juvy say "Back that ass up," it was on.

Jaz was getting her groove on when she looked up and saw Faheem coming her way. As he headed over, this female grabbed him and whispered in his ear. Faheem grinned and shook his head. He pointed at Jaz. The girl snapped her neck and looked Jaz up and down. Jaz winked at her and kept dancing. The female gave it one more try, whispering something else in Faheem's ear. Faheem blushed and left the pouting sister on the dance floor.

"Excuse me, partna. Can I cut in?" Faheem was staring at Smooth.

Jaz kept dancing, watching Faheem. Smooth looked at Faheem, then at Jaz.

"Can't you wait until this song is over, bro?" Smooth said.

"Fuck, no. I can't wait. This is my woman you all up on."

Jaz knew that shit was about to get out of hand. She tried to calm everybody down.

"Smooth, this is my man Faheem. Baby, this is Smooth. He balls for the Nets. We was just talkin' about Princeton, 'cause he graduated from there and we took a lot of the same classes."

Faheem just stared at Smooth.

"Take care, Jaz," Smooth said. "Thanks for the dance." As he turned to walk away, he mouthed the words, *I'll call you.*

"See, this is just the reason I don't like to go out. These niggas will have me sittin' on a murder charge," Faheem said.

"Faheem, baby, why you got to come in here trying to trip?" She gave him a hug.

"I ain't trippin'. Niggas just need to know when to step, that's all."

"If you wasn't looking so good, I would've kept dancing with that baller," she joked. He was wearing a black leather baggy jumpsuit. The zipper was down, showing his smooth chest and his iced necklace with the initials FM. He had a big rock in his left ear and an iced up Rolex. It looked like he just came from the barber, with a fresh cut and trimmed mustache. He wore the Carolina Herrera cologne that she bought him. She couldn't help but put a passion mark on his chest. Luther was starting to heat up the atmosphere, blowing "A House Is Not A Home." Faheem pulled Jaz close and caressed her behind as they danced.

"Baby, you look so fine," she said as she rubbed his chest.

"You do, too, even though you out here half naked." He sniffed her hair and then kissed her on the neck. "You smell good, too."

"So do you. How long have you been here? I was hoping you would come."

"Bout an hour. I told you I had some business to take of. I brought Brian with me. He wanted to see your sister." Brian was the daddy of Micki's five-year-old, Misa.

"Brian introduced me to your sister. She is all the way live."

"I told you," Jaz said. "Why he come here looking for her? He couldn't wait until she got home to talk to her?"

"I don't know, baby. It ain't my business."

"I hope they don't start no shit up in here."

"He seems cool. He said he want to make it right with her and be a father to his daughter."

"That would be a good thing. Even though he waited five years."

They both got quiet and closed their eyes. Jagged Edge was singing "Promise" and Faheem was singing along softly in Jaz's ear. She had put two more passion marks on his chest. The longer they slow danced, the harder his dick got.

"Damn, baby. Let's sneak off somewhere." He was holding her tight, kissing her all over her neck.

"I can't leave my girls here. That wouldn't be right."

"We'll only be gone for fifteen minutes. They won't miss us," he whispered into her ear.

"You can't wait until we get home?"

"Baby, my dick is hard now." He opened his eyes and was looking dead at Smooth. "Damn! What you say to that nigga? He standing over there watching me feel your ass. Niggas like him want to get respect but they don't know how to give it. I would be wrong if I went over there and smoked his ass."

Faheem broke away from Jaz and headed toward Smooth. A big vein was popping across his forehead, and Jaz knew that meant he was heated.

"No, Faheem!" Jaz pulled him back. "Ignore him. He ain't nobody. Dance with me. This is the jam." Mystikal was screaming "Danger! Danger! Get on the floor!" Jaz danced close up on Faheem and laughed.

"Why you gotta act all jealous? I don't act like that when I see these females sweatin' you. As long as we don't disrespect each other, then it's all good. You fine as hell, Faheem. I know they gonna try you. Like that bitch who was whispering in your ear. Who was that?"

"Somebody I used to fuck with."

"What she want?"

"She wanted me to fuck her."

"Mm-hm." Jaz crossed her arms over her chest. "See what I mean?"

"I told her my woman was right over here. That's why I pointed at you. Jaz, do we supposed to be groovin' or playin' 20 questions?"

"Twenty questions, baby," she answered as she bounced to "Can I Get What What."

"Okay, then why you give that nigga your number? I saw him say I'll call you."

"'Cause we took some of the same classes at the same school and he bought me a drink. I was just being polite. I only gave him my pager. Plus, I told him you was my man." Jaz grinned and rubbed all up on Faheem.

"You know you wrong, right?" Faheem said as he grooved to the music. He was just as good as Jaz on the dance floor. They looked good together.

"When he page you, you better not call him back."

"Oh, so it's like that, huh?"

"Yup, it's like that. I'm trying to look out for you."

"And how is that?"

"All that nigga wanna do is hit it and run. You'll be lying there pissed off, feeling guilty, and then you'll be crawling back, asking me to take you back."

"Faheem, you're fulla shit. You know that, right?"

"Nah, baby, I'm dead serious. Don't fuck with me, Jaz."

"What up, Faheem? Good to see you, man!" Someone came up behind them and shouted. Faheem turned around and smiled.

"What up, Buju?" He grabbed the brother and they hugged. "This my woman, Jaz. Jaz this is my partna, Buju." Buju grabbed Jaz's hand and kissed it.

"Faheem, call me. I got business to discuss." Faheem nodded at him and Buju disappeared into the crowd.

"Where your girls at?" Faheem asked Jaz as he grabbed her hand and pulled her off the dance floor.

Jaz looked around. "It's no telling where they are."

"Come on!" Faheem kept pulling her.

"Faheem, dance with me," she whined.

"Dance? Baby, I want some pussy. We can run to the limo real quick." He wouldn't let go of Jaz's hand as he looked around for her girls. He spotted Brian and Micki and started grinning.

"Yo, Brian!" He was heading for their table and literally dragging Jaz behind him. Brian and Micki were having a serious conversation. They looked up when Jaz and Faheem were standing beside the table.

"Yo, look after Angel and Roz for a few." Faheem told Brian. "We'll be back in twenty minutes."

Brian nodded and then looked at Jaz.

"What's up, Brian?" Jaz asked him. But before he could say anything, Faheem was pulling her through the crowd.

They barely had the door to the limo closed when Faheem started tonguing Jaz down. He laid her back on the leather seat and reached up under her skirt. Her thong came off in one swift motion. He could feel how wet she was, and he couldn't wait to get up in there. He pulled down her tube top and went to work on her hard nipples.

"Do you have some protection, Faheem?"

"Naw." He stopped sucking for a second to answer her. "You ain't got none?"

"Faheem. Don't start. You knew you was coming; why don't you carry them with you? Why is that so hard for you to do?"

"Why would I be carrying some protection? I wasn't planning on fucking nobody on the way up here."

"You was planning on fucking me!" Jaz yelled. She was getting mad. "I told you I'm not trying to get pregnant right now. Why can't you respect that?" She pushed him up off her.

"Shit!" Faheem spat. He looked at Jaz to see if she was gonna give in. From the expression on her face, she wasn't budging.

"We can wait until we get home, Faheem," she told him.

144

"This is your pussy. It ain't going nowhere." She kissed him and he took the opportunity to slide two fingers inside her while he sucked on her tongue.

"Faheem, baby, not without some latex," she moaned.

Faheem pulled his fingers out and she watched him taste her juices.

"Damn, baby," he said. "Sit tight." He went up to the front of the limo and banged on the glass.

"Yo, Akbar!" He banged again. The window came down some and Faheem mumbled something to the driver. The driver said something back and Faheem pulled his wallet to give the man some money. Akbar put something into Faheem's hand, closed the partition and got out of the car. Faheem climbed back to Jaz with a grin.

"Take off everything," he commanded.

"Faheem!"

"Come on, baby. The doors are locked, the windows are tinted. We straight. I paid him to stand guard outside. I wanna hear you holler, baby."

He slid out of his jumpsuit and gave Jaz the latex to put on him. He laid her down and raised one of her legs into the crook of his arm, plunging into her until he hit bottom.

Jaz moaned in pleasure as their motion rocked the limo back and forth. The harder her nails dug into his back, the harder he would grind, and the louder she would holler.

"Bring it on, baby," he whispered in her ear, and she let it go, hollering his name the whole time. Then Faheem let go, shaking and quivering as he called her name.

As they lay there holding each other, Faheem said, "Whose pussy is this?"

"It belongs to Faheem," she whispered in his ear.

"Can I bust another nut?" he asked her as he stroked her hair.

"Sure, but let's go home and get in the bed."

"Bet." He kissed her and climbed up off her.

Jaz was glad the limo had a bar with a faucet and some clean towels. They cleaned themselves off, got dressed and went back into the club. They both had satisfied grins on their faces. They went back to the table with Brian and Micki. Brian told them that Angel and Roz were still partying.

"Come on, Micki. I'm ready to go." Jaz yawned. "I got homework."

"I'm not," Micki said as she looked over at Brian.

"Yo, Brian, you take the limo," Faheem said.

"Me and my baby, we outta here."

"I'll hold it down, man. Thanks, man." He stood up and grabbed Faheem.

Jaz hugged Micki. "Welcome home, big sis. I'll holler at you tomorrow. Make sure them two hoochies don't get into no trouble."

Micki laughed as she watched her sister leave, hanging onto Faheem like he was made of gold.

Chapter 21

The next day was Saturday. Jaz got up and cooked Faheem breakfast, cleaned up his apartment, gathered his dirty laundry and went home. Faheem owned the house that Jaz called her home. Faheem would float back and forth between his apartment and the house.

Jaz planned to stay inside the whole weekend. She had a ton of homework, not to mention she had to clean her own house and do laundry for her and Faheem. She didn't speak to anyone all day Saturday, but Faheem woke her Sunday morning with the sound of his keys landing on her glass coffee table.

"I hate it when he does that," she mumbled. Faheem came into the bedroom and dove on top of her.

"Ooww!" she yelled and punched Faheem on his arm. "Why you gotta play so early in the morning?"

"Baby, it's almost noon." He kissed her stomach. "How come you didn't come over last night?"

"I told you I had two papers to write. I'm still not finished. Now let me up so I can brush my teeth and wash my face." Faheem got up, took off his jacket and threw it on the arm of the chair.

"You want me to help you with your homework?"

"I wish you could."

"I ran into Marvin last night. He's glad he's having a baby."

"How do you know he's glad?" she asked, trying to floss at the same time.

"'Cause he said so. He's talking about moving to Cali. Said ain't shit happening in Jersey."

"He's taking Kyra to Cali?" Jaz peeked her head out of the doorway.

"That's his woman. Why wouldn't he take her?"

"Damn. I wonder when was she planning on telling somebody."

"I also ran into Tyler's brother Ahmad."

"Where was you at, a ballers convention?"

Faheem ignored that comment. "You know their baby brother got killed?"

Jaz came out of the bathroom, wiping her face. "Who? Lil' Anthony? How?"

"Yeah, Lil' Anthony. You know he was always stealing cars just to be joyridin' and shit. He stole a Camaro and the police chased his ass all around the East Side. They were chasing him for about 40 minutes, then he jumped on Route 29 doing about a hundred. Sideswiped three cars before he slid under a moving tractor trailer. Took the top of the car off and they say his head, too. Then it caught on fire. Ahmad is fucked up about that shit. He lost two brothers in one year."

"Dayum! Kyra was crazy bout Lil' Anthony. I gotta call her." Jaz went to the phone next to her bed and started dialing. The phone kept ringing. Jaz hung up, then decided to page her. She picked up the phone again. Faheem left the bedroom when Kyra called right back. He knew they'd probably be on the phone for a while.

He let Jaz and Kyra talk for about an hour before he hit the remote and went back into the bedroom. As Jaz stood next to the bed and talked on the phone, she watched Faheem take off his clothes. She still didn't hang up when he came over and slid off her negligee and matching panties. He sat on the side of the bed and ran his hand slowly up and down her thighs. Jaz turned around to face him and he reached between her legs to massage her clit. She stifled a moan, but she kept talking to Kyra. Faheem liked watching the pleasure on her face as he slid three fingers deep inside her. When he found her G-spot, Jaz shuddered and released a stream of juices.

"I gotta go, girl," she told Kyra, then hung up without waiting for a response.

"Do that again," she told Faheem, her voice trembling with passion.

Faheem swirled his tongue around her erect nipples as he massaged her G-spot again. He was making her scream with pleasure. She dug her nails into his shoulders as she came again. Faheem didn't stop. He kept working her until she finally collapsed against him, trembling and crying. He loved to see her this way. Faheem knew he was the shit.

"You okay, baby?" He looked up at her with a smile. "That's what you get for not coming over last night."

"Oh, yeah?" Jaz said. "Well I got something for you, too."

She pushed him back on the bed, tucked a pillow under his head and began stroking and squeezing his dick. He put both hands behind his head to watch her. Jaz lowered her head and wrapped her lips around Faheem's dick. He closed his eyes and started moaning.

"Baby, that feels good," he whispered. Jaz responded by swallowing him as far into her throat as she could get it.

He was trembling when he hollered, "Whoa baby, don't make

me bust a nut yet!" She eased up, and looked up at his face. His dick was standing straight up when she straddled him and slid down on his long pole, nice and slow. Just when he hit bottom, she pulled it out. She kept teasing him by sliding on and off it. The more she did it, the harder it got. When he couldn't take anymore, he grabbed her butt and held her down tight. He gave a good thrust to get in as deep as possible, then started rocking her back and forth until she had an orgasm that seemed like it would never stop. Finally, she collapsed on top of him.

Faheem let her rest for a few, then he flipped her over and placed kisses all over her body. She moaned and groaned, telling him how much she loved him. He was still hard as a rock, so he pulled her up onto her hands and knees and slid it in from behind. He massaged her ass and smiled to himself. Her moistness felt so good, and he was glad she hadn't mentioned anything about latex. He loved the way she felt without it, and though he didn't tell her, Faheem wanted Jaz to have his baby.

"Whose pussy is this?" he whispered in her ear as he pumped her doggy-style.

"It's yours, Faheem," she moaned.

"Don't you ever forget that shit." He told her, then he gave it one last push and busted a big nut.

Chapter 22

Jaz was sitting in her organic chemistry class on Monday morning when her pager started to vibrate. She looked at the number but didn't recognize it. She figured it was probably Faheem, out somewhere. She waited until after class to dial the number from her cell phone.

"Hello?" A male voice said.

"This is Jaz. Who is this?"

"I know who you are. I can't get that voice outta my head. This is Smooth."

Jaz's eyes got wide. She knew she'd given him the pager number, but she didn't really think he'd call, and definitely not so soon.

"Hey, what's up?" she finally said.

"I'm checking to see what's up with you."

"I'm getting ready to hit my quantitative analysis class."

"That course is a motherfucker! You trying to get it done, huh?"

"Yeah. I'm trying. It ain't easy."

"Tell me about it," Smooth said. "Listen, I'm in the area and I was wondering if I could treat you to lunch."

"Thanks, but not today. Mondays are full for me. I'll have to take a raincheck."

"A'ight. Can I get your home number?"

"I'm rarely home, Smooth. And when I am, you remember Faheem, right? Well, he's always there. So, no, you can't have my number."

"How serious is it between you and him? I didn't see no rock on your finger, so it can't be all that serious."

"Oh, he got the rock. I haven't put it on yet." *This nigga gotta lot of nerve*, she thought.

"Well, if you was mines, you wouldn't even be hesitating to put it on."

I ain't got to explain myself to this nigga.

"Is that so?" she said with attitude.

"Yeah. That is so. I'll hit you up again."

Jaz closed up her cell phone and went on to her next class. She thought nothing of the phone conversation as she plopped down next to Brett Dumont, a white nerd who had been in almost all of her classes for the last two and a half years. They were both working on a chemistry major.

"What's up, Brett?"

"These fucking term papers, Jasmine."

"Tell me about it."

"You'll be ready after class?"

"Yeah. I'll be ready. I'll meet you out front."

After class, Jaz hit the ladies' room and the snack machine before she went outside. Brett was parked out front, sitting on the hood of his Chevy Impala with an open book in his lap. When he looked up and saw Jaz coming, he got down and gathered up his belongings.

Every Monday and Thursday Jaz went with Brett somewhere in the boondocks deep down in Jersey or Pennsylvania. She would never know where they were headed until they were on their way. Jaz was a cook. She and Brett cooked up crank, or crystal meth, by the pound. Crank is a speed that keeps the user up for days, and white folks loved it. That shit was big money.

Jaz cooked twice a week, at twelve grand per day. She didn't have to sell it. She and Brett would cook it, pack it, then he would pay her in cash. They would jump in the car and go, so she never knew how the meth was being distributed on the streets. She assumed that someone else would come and pick it up.

Jaz never told anyone what she was doing for extra money, not even her girls and especially not Faheem. Brett was the only person who knew, and she was glad. She felt a little bad about what she did, but she was at least glad that she was not selling to her people. The shit was flooding the white neighborhoods, and she was able to stash twenty-four grand a week, hoping to use some of the money to retire her parents to a nice, big house down South someday. Her chemistry major was already paying off big time, and she hadn't even graduated yet.

Jaz usually fell asleep while Brett drove. This day was no different. When the car finally stopped, she sat up, yawned and stretched.

"Time to make the donuts!" Brett joked. She grabbed her book bag with her change of clothes and they went inside. They worked for hours and at the end of the night, Jaz pocketed another twelve grand.

"Now, please hurry up and get me out of these fuckin' boondocks," she said to Brett, and they both laughed. By the time Brett dropped her off in front of the school to pick up her car, it was almost 10:00 P.M. She had to wait until morning to stash her money.

The next morning, Jaz's pager vibrated again during class.

This time she recognized the number. It was Smooth again. She decided it was time to tell him to stop paging her, 'cause ain't nothing happening. She called him.

"What's up, Smooth?"

"Guess where I'm at?"

"Back at the club in New York?" she joked, hoping that he was far away.

"Naw, I'm right out front. I told you I want to take you to lunch. Wherever you want to go."

"That won't be a good thing, Smooth."

"Why not? It's just lunch. Plus, you could pick my brain for those two exams you got coming up. Kill two birds with one stone."

"You just made me an offer I can't refuse. I'll be right out."

When Jaz got out front he was standing by his car signing autographs. When he looked up and saw her coming, he left his fans and approached her.

"Damn, girl! You look fine even in baggy jeans and a sweatshirt," he said as he hugged her.

"I feel like a bum. Look at you, Armani down. I knew I should have declined your invitation." She looked him up and down and noticed that he really was fine. That dark club didn't do him any justice.

"I'm not letting you back out. Look, I'll lose the jacket and the tie." He took them both off and laid them in the trunk. "Give me your books." He put them in the trunk, too. "Now, is this better?"

"Not really."

He smiled and opened the car door for her.

"Nice ride," she told him. It was a Benz convertible, a navy blue two-seater. It had beige Coach leather seats and navy blue carpet.

"Where do you want to go?" He looked at her and smiled.

Jaz thought about it. "Let's go to the Hyatt on Route 1. I love their key lime pie."

"No problem." Smooth was being the perfect gentleman. Opening up doors, pulling out chairs. Jaz enjoyed his company as they talked about Princeton and all the classes he had taken that she was taking now. In between his meal of mushroom chicken and marinated asparagus salad, Smooth had to stop a few times to sign autographs for fans who stopped by their table. Jaz watched how much he loved the attention as she ate her sesame fish and gingered spinach. They both had the key lime pie for dessert.

When lunch was over, neither one of them was ready to say good-bye. Jaz invited Smooth over to her place so she could pick his brain about upcoming term papers and assignments. Smooth took her back to the school to get her Escalade, then he followed her home.

They worked for three hours straight on her chemistry term paper. Smooth got on the Internet and showed her all the hot spots for the research she needed to do. They had books and papers scattered everywhere. The brother wasn't a dummy, and Jaz was grateful for his help.

"Oh, my God," she said as she looked at the time. "I didn't know we'd been working so long. Can I at least get you something to drink?" she said.

"Whatever you have," he answered. Jaz came back with two Tropicana Twisters, and they plopped on the couch together. It wasn't long before Smooth leaned over and tried to kiss Jaz.

"Look, Smooth," she said as she pushed him away. "I ain't like those hoochies falling all over you at the restaurant. Just 'cause you a ball player don't mean I want to fuck you. I appreciate your help with my term paper and all, but I already told you I got a man, and he gives me everything I need, thank you." What she didn't tell him was that if she wasn't Faheem's woman, it would definitely be on.

"I want you to come to my next game." Smooth wasn't about to give up.

"I don't think so."

"Why not?"

"You're not used to rejection, are you?"

Jaz's jaw dropped when she heard keys jingling in the front door lock. Before she could say anything, Faheem walked in the room.

"Aw, shit!" She stood up and put some distance between her and Smooth.

Faheem threw the keys on the glass table. "Hey, baby." He looked at Smooth, then back at Jaz.

"What's up? You aiight, or am I interrupting something in my own motherfuckin' house?" He kept his gaze locked on Smooth, who had a smirk on his face.

"We were working on my term papers and researching info on the Internet. You remember Smooth, right, baby?" Her heart was racing. "He was just leaving."

Faheem's nose was flaring and that big vein popped up on his forehead. He looked at Smooth.

"You that nigga from the club," he said angrily. "How the fuck you gonna disrespect me like this, man?" He reached behind his back and pulled out his .44. When he saw Smooth reach for his jacket, he cocked it and pressed the barrel against his forehead.

"Faheem!" Jaz screamed. "What is the matter with you? We was working, baby!" She stepped back and started crying. "You crazy, Faheem!"

Faheem was seeing blood and didn't hear a word she said.

"Answer me, motherfucker! How you gonna be all up in a nigga's house?"

"Look, man, the bitch invited me over. What would you—"

Faheem cracked him in the head with the butt of the gun and then punched him in the mouth. Jaz was now screaming hysterically. Faheem hit Smooth in the mouth again and liked it when he saw the blood running down his chin.

"Get the fuck outta my house." He put the gun back in his face and said, "This is your lucky day. One, because I don't want your fuckin' blood all over my house, and two, because this bitch is a witness. That's the only reason I won't blow your fuckin' brains out, G."

Smooth staggered out the front door. Faheem slammed the door and locked it. Jaz stood crying in the middle of the room.

"Faheem, we wasn't doing nothing!" He put his gun away. "Studying, my ass, Jaz. Do you think I'm stupid?" he yelled.

"I swear, Faheem!" She was trembling, scared of what Faheem might do next. "You're crazy, Faheem." She collapsed onto the couch.

"Why the fuck you got a nigga up in my crib? You the one who's fuckin' crazy!" He picked up the coffee table and dumped everything off it. Juice, glasses, books and papers. He grabbed the lamp and tossed it at the wall.

"Stop it, Faheem!" she screamed.

"Why you had to fuckin' play me like that, Jaz? I told you not to call that nigga! How long you been fuckin' him?" He was standing over her with his fist balled up.

"I didn't fuck him, Faheem! I swear!" she screamed. The tears were pouring down her face. "You know I would never hurt you like that."

"Yeah, right."

"Faheem, baby."

He ignored her and went and looked in the bathroom for evidence that this bitch was lying. He didn't even care that he didn't find anything.

"I don't believe this shit!" he grabbed his keys off the floor. "Come get your shit out of my apartment by tonight and leave my fuckin' keys on the fuckin' dresser. Whatever you don't pick up, it's going outside in the fuckin' trash." He walked out the door, slamming it so hard the front windowpane cracked.

"Faheem!" Jaz got up and ran to the door. "I didn't fuck him!" she screamed.

Faheem slammed down his trunk, jumped in his Jag and sped off. Jaz cried until she had no more tears left and her throat was raw.

Chapter 23

My brothers, I can't believe this shit! I ain't gonna try to front. I'm all fucked up. This is how it went down. My dick is hard, so I go to my woman's house to get me some pussy. I walk in the door and she got some punk-ass ball-playing mother-fucker sitting all up on my shit. I tried to be cool. I tried not to lose it. But I lost it. Then he had the nerve to call her a bitch and say she invited him over. Shit, I know the game. I still got my player's card in my wallet. Fuck, I got a fuckin' plaque hangin' on my wall! I swear, I could've blown his fuckin' brains out right then and there.

I know Jaz. I done spoiled the bitch. I know she ain't fuck him, but it's the principle of the thing. They both were fully dressed, books and papers were all over the place and the computer was on. I even checked the bedroom and the bathroom. Everything was straight. I still lost it. Like I said, it's the principle of the thing. Just the thought of some other nigga going up into mines gives me the fuckin' creeps.

I can't believe she played me like that. I make sure she don't want for nothing. That house is mines. I let her have it. I live in a fuckin' apartment. The Escalade, I paid for that. She don't

159

have to worry about me bringing no diseases home or disrespecting her. Bitches don't be calling the house or none of that shit. I never even hit her. I wanted to today, though. But I didn't. I just threw shit around.

You know what? I'm glad this shit happened. She need to be taught a lesson. If a nigga is good to you, you don't play him. You love him, respect him and give him some babies who love him and respect him. That's the way I was taught. Then it's an added bonus if your nigga can push all the right buttons. I make sure she come two or three times before I even get one. Ain't too many niggas gonna do that for a bitch. Shit, ain't nothin' I wouldn't do for her.

I remember when she finally let me take her out. We went to the club. We had a good time. We was really feelin' each other. When I took her home I parked in front of her crib. She was real direct.

I said, "I want you to be my woman."

She looked at me and got all serious.

"I want to be your woman, but you got to be able to take care of me without being in the game. You're smart and ambitious, not to mention you are fine. I've been watching you. Plus, I heard that you can fuck real good and that you got a hurricane tongue."

"That's what you heard, huh? I don't know from where."

"C'mon, Faheem. You know you gets around, so stop playing the innocent role."

"Yeah, but that getting around, that shit gets real old after a while."

"I can't tell."

"Trust me. It does."

"So, what are you saying?"

"I'm saying, I'm ready to chill out with you, and you alone. And I want to know if you could chill with me and me alone."

"Yes, I can."

"Well, let's do it."

"I told you. Whoever I chill with won't be in the game. I can't spend my time with someone for a year or two, worryin' if he's gonna get snatched up and sent to prison for twenty years. That's a waste of my time and energy. My heart couldn't take it."

I thought about that for a while.

"Why are you so quiet? Can't do it, can you?"

"I'm just thinking, that's all. I'm a step ahead of you. I'm already working on getting out. My pops is in prison. My brother and two of my uncles are locked down. I know them mafuckas got a cell waitin' on my ass. I'm trying, Jaz. I'm trying."

"Well, Faheem. It's on you now. I will wait for you, but not forever. Just come and get me when you're ready. Now, unlock the door."

"Oh, it's like that, huh?"

"I told you. I'll be ready to commit, and I'll wait for you to get your shit together. How long I'll wait, I don't know. I had fun tonight, but I got to get up early. I got a class at eight."

"Can I get a kiss, so that I'll at least know what I got waitin' for me?"

"Unlock the door first, just in case you might wanna try something."

I leaned over and kissed her. A kiss that lasted almost five minutes.

"Mmm, Jaz." I rubbed her thigh. "Let me taste you."

"You already did," she said, looking straight in my eyes.

"You know what I'm talking about," I told her as I raised her skirt.

"Oh, you think you smooth like that, huh? You go down on every female on the first date? So I guess the rumors are true."

"Nah. You can't believe everything you hear. I'm only going down on you because you said you wanted to be my woman and you would commit, and I know you ain't lying. Plus, I want to give you a damn good reason to wait for me."

"Oh, it's like that?"

"Yeah, it's like that."

She leaned back against the door and I spread her thighs so my tongue could work its magic. It didn't take long before I had her moaning and groaning, trying to climb to the roof of the car. She grabbed my head and came long and hard, all over my face. Damn, she tasted good.

"Yeah, you definitely worth a nigga walking the straight and narrow." I unlocked the door for her.

"You don't know how bad I want to fuck you. Don't keep me waiting too long," she told me as she got out the car.

That girl had my head fucked up after that. It took me almost two years to turn shit over and over good enough to have something to sit on and open the liquor stores. Then I went and got her. I guess she gave up on me, 'cause I had to take her from this nigga Sabu. He wasn't shit. Nigga ain't know how to handle a woman like her. She looked at me like I was a knight in shining armor.

Now, look at this dumb shit she done went and pulled.

She just want to finish school before she give me a baby. But I want a baby now. Because after she gets her Bachelor's degree, she going for her Master's. And knowing her, then she'll be on for her Ph.D. I say fuck that, we gotta have babies in between.

She ain't gotta work nowhere, and she can still keep going to school. That's why I don't be wearing no protection whenever I can get away with it.

So, what am I gonna do now? A lesson must be taught. I'ma punish her ass.

Chapter 24

Well, my sisters, I know most of you are probably saying that I fucked up big time. Let curiosity get the best of me. I knew I should have followed my gut feelings and told Smooth to stop paging me. I should have never called him back. That ho had the nerve to call me a bitch. He better not let me catch his ass nowhere. I don't care what team he play for. All I did was go to a simple lunch with him. We came back to the crib, put a big-ass dent in my backlog of assignments and drank some juice. We talked, he told me about the contract he signed with the Nets and he did kiss me once. But that's all I let him do. He begged me for a taste, but I told him I don't allow taste tests.

I definitely couldn't go there. That would be suicide, knowing that Faheem has a key and could walk in at any moment. I was adamant. No can do! Homeboy got game, but I ain't crazy. Faheem act like he got a built-in radar that'll tell him if I fucked somebody or not. That nigga is crazy. You see how he acted. Imagine if he woulda caught us doing something—we both would have been dead. Plus, I couldn't and wouldn't dog Faheem out like that. I'm crazy about him, and he is too good to me. I don't have any complaints other than him throwing his keys on my glass table. He gives me my space and he is the shit in the bed-room. I do love him a whole lot, and he would be the man who I'd marry. He's responsible, he's smart, he's a provider, and he's fine as hell and he knows it.

This was the first time I ever saw him in a rage. He was mad as hell. I was crouched on the sofa, praying *Please God, don't let this nigga hit me.* Now I feel sick at the thought of losing him over some bullshit.

After I cleaned up the mess that Faheem made, I paged Angel, Roz, and Kyra. I needed guidance and moral fuckin' support. Everyone called me right back. In between sobs I told them what all happened. Roz called me a dumb bitch. Kyra gave me a lec-ture on treating your man the way you would want to be treated. She got a lot of fuckin' nerve. At least I didn't bone him while Faheem was in the next room sleep! Angel called me a stupid-ass whore and told me to throw myself on the ground in front of him and beg for forgiveness. She also volunteered to go with me to get my stuff from his apartment. She said one good thing is that if he really thought I fucked him, he would have put me out of his house, put my ass on the street. Faheem don't play. The nigga is sweet, but he can act crazy.

So I went and got my shit out of his apartment and I prayed that Angel was right. Maybe he really did believe me. I just had to wait out his little punishment, and sooner or later he'd call me. I just didn't know how long he would make me wait.

Chapter 25

It had been two weeks since Jaz emptied her things from Faheem's apartment and left the keys on his dresser. In that time, Jaz waited patiently for Faheem to contact her. Smooth kept blowing up her pager, but she refused to call him back. She was not about to speak to no brother who called her a bitch, fine or not.

When she couldn't take Faheem's silence anymore, she tried to contact him. He refused to answer her pages, no matter how many times she tried. When she called his cell, he would hang up as soon as he heard her voice. After a while he just turned off the ringer. Her only choice then was to go by his liquor stores and try to talk to him in person. But he knew she would do that sooner or later, so he'd already told his employees not to let her back to see him.

After a while, she just gave up. All the time and energy she was spending trying to talk to Faheem was time she could have been spending on her schoolwork. The semester would be over in another month, and she did not want to fuck up her grades now. So she started spending all her time either at school, or with her sister Micki.

She was glad to know that Micki was adjusting pretty well to the free world. She had found part-time clerical work at Motor Vehicles and had moved out of her mother's house and in with her grandmother, who lived in the projects. Micki said her mother's house was too crowded, even though their parents' home had six bedrooms.

Along with their parents, Glenda and Jack Taylor, Micki and her three kids had to share the house with her brother Darien and two of his kids, her sister Tanisha and her two boys, and her brother Punk Eddy, who had AIDS. Micki told Jaz the main reason she had to get out of that house was because she couldn't stand to be around Punk Eddy, and Jaz understood why.

When Eddy was twelve years old, six members of this gang called Notorious Philly Hoods was threatening to kick his ass. To divert the ass whipping, he took them to the house. He held down Micki, who was only ten years old, while all six of the Hoods raped her. As if that wasn't enough, he let all six of them do him, too. That's where the name Punk Eddy came from. When their cousin Juwan found out, he beat Eddy until he almost died. Punk Eddy wasn't right in the head since.

Micki had never been able to forgive or forget. That rape was the real reason she started using and selling crack, and ended up doing a five-year bid at Clinton. Even though she had been attending counseling sessions while locked up, Jaz could tell her sister was still hurting. Jaz prayed that her sister would be able to heal, for the sake of her kids.

Jaz had just spent the day with Micki and her kids, and she was exhausted. Those kids were enough to wear anybody out. It was past 11:00, so she took a quick shower and headed for bed. She had an early class in the morning.

A while later, Jaz thought she was still dreaming when she heard the familiar sound of Faheem's keys hitting the glass table.

Then she heard him say "Damn!" when he bumped into the TV, and she knew she was awake. She turned on the night lamp and looked at the clock. It said 2:47 A.M. but she didn't care what time it was. She was so happy to see Faheem when he walked into the bedroom.

He had on a deep blue Armani suit, and his cologne lit up the room. She sat up in the bed and watched while he went to the closet and pulled out a box. He combed through it in silence. He put the box back in the closet and took off his navy blue Gators.

"Faheem, baby. How long do you plan on being mad at me?"

"Jaz. Not now." He didn't even look at her.

"Then when, Faheem?" He ignored her and began taking off his clothes, throwing everything on the chair. He got completely naked, fell on top of the covers and went to sleep. He was lying flat on his stomach, with the back of his head facing Jaz. She ran her eyes over his dark brown, naked body and thought about how much she missed him. She turned out the night lamp and snuggled up next to him.

"Faheem, I'm sorry," she whispered as she kissed his neck. "I didn't fuck him, and I'll never hurt you again. I am so sorry." She cried herself back to sleep. When she woke up later that morning, Faheem was already gone. She started crying again and called Angel.

"He didn't smell like perfume?"

"Nope," Jaz said, sniffling.

"Damn. Dayum! He played you like that? He got butt naked and just went to sleep? He didn't even cover up?"

"Nope." Still sniffling.

"Dayum! He wanted you to see what you've been missing. You didn't even get a kiss? No conversation? Nothing?"

"Nope."

"Why didn't you just take it?"

"He was sleep, Angel. Plus, he's still pissed."

"I don't know what to tell you. What are you gonna do?"

"I don't know. I don't know what he wants me to do. He's stressing me the fuck out. He's treating me like I fucked the nigga when I didn't."

"No, not really," Angel said. "I told you, if he thought you fucked Smooth, he would've put your ass out of his house, took the car and closed your bank account. Didn't he open a bank account for you?"

"What's that got to do with anything?"

"Jaz, please stop crying. Concentrate on finishing up this semester. He'll come around eventually. Wait it out. Plus, remember you the one had that nigga all up in his house. You should've gotten a nerd to help you out, but you had to go get a fine-ass ballplayer with loot! You was wrong for that. That was a crackhead move."

"Fuck you, Angel."

"You want the truth, don't you? And stop crying! You gettin' me depressed. At least he came home. You ain't all the way in the doghouse."

"What if he's seeing somebody else?"

"I doubt it. You got that nigga sprung. Look how he actin'! Snap out of it and keep busy. Okay?"

"Okay."

"Now go take your dumb ass to class."

Chapter 26

I can't believe that it's close to a month now since Faheem has been giving me the silent treatment. I have to say, though, I've been handling it much better. After he did that shit that night he came by and wouldn't touch me, I've been keeping my head buried in the books. The only time I do something other than study is to see my nieces and nephews or to make my Monday and Thursday runs with Brett. But even that's gonna change soon. Those chemicals are starting to make me sick. I told Brett again that at the end of this semester, I'm out.

It's Thursday. My stomach is cramping but nothing is coming down. No period. I've been stressing too much. I'm tired and irritable. When class is over, I would love to go home and crawl under the covers. Plus, it's pouring down rain. But happy-ass surfer dude Brett said he'll meet me out front. What can I say? A deal's a deal. I reiterate to him that after this semester, the chef is hanging up her apron. He's going to have to find someone else. I got a nice stash. Don't be greedy and you won't get swallowed up. Plus, I've been lucky that Faheem hasn't found out about this.

I only did this as long as I have because I have big plans. My mom and dad want to move back to Alabama with their family. I don't blame them. For their 30th anniversary, I'm going to surprise them with a house down there. Pack 'em up and ship 'em out. They need to get away from all this madness up here. Go someplace where they can retire and die in peace. Leave the house and its problems to all them folks living in it.

Anyway, now I'm talking to all you hustlers. You know how it feels when you out there doing the shit you do to get paid and you get this gut feeling that something ain't right? You can't put your finger on it, but you feel funny and you nix it. Tell yourself it's paranoia. That's how I feel today. Me and Brett are headed toward PA. The scenery is nice and relaxing but he's blastin' a fuckin' Limp Bizkit CD. I would rather listen to what I got—the blues.

We finally pull up to this house with what seems like a two-mile driveway. I grab my change of clothes and we go inside. We're only inside about thirty minutes and I hear cars rolling up.

"Yo, Brett! You expectin' somebody?" He pulls off his rubber gloves, looks out the window and screams, "Oh, shit! It's a fuckin' raid! Dump this shit!"

So we running around pouring, dumping, and flushing shit down the toilet. Them motherfuckers are bangin' on the doors. They got the house surrounded. You know how they roll. FBI, ATF, DEA, local police, sheriff's office, and if the fire department can squeeze in, they'll join the party, too. They break the door in, screaming, hollering, cussing at us, telling us to lie face-down on the floor, hands behind our backs and don't fuckin' move or they'll blow our brains out. Then they're taking me away. This is why I was feeling so weird all day. I should have took my ass home. Playing the game, you never know when, but it's always when you least expect it.

We pull up to a jail in Pennsylvania. I don't know which one it is. For whatever reason, I'm not welcome, and now we're headed to the funky-ass Mercer County Jail in downtown Trenton. I'm disappointed, because at least the Pennsylvania jail looked clean. Mercer County Jail, that's another story. The building looks nice on the outside, but on the inside it looks like something from another century. The jail part, anyhow.

By the time they get me processed, it's almost 2 A.M. They won't let me use the phone. They hand me a raggedy jean-like nightgown and lock me in my cell. I can't believe this shit!

"Taylor! Get up if you need any medication. The pill cart is here. Taylor!" This person is shaking the bars now. Damn. I was hoping that this was a nightmare. "You missed breakfast. It's served at 6:30," she says as she lets me out of my cell.

"What time is it?" I ask this lady in a uniform with a gigantic butt and ran-over shoes.

"Clock's on the wall," she says and keeps on going. Damn. It's 9:45 A.M.

"Can I use the phone? I didn't get my one phone call."

"Phone's over there!"

"Excuse me, can I get a washcloth, soap and a toothbrush?" The bitch just keeps right on walking.

"Hi, I'm Michelle." Some white girl, looking like a crackhead, says to me.

"Who gives a fuck," I answer her.

"You got a cigarette?"

I ignore her and walk down the metal stairs to where the phones are. The TV is blasting and there are several card games going on. Half the place is sleep, but it's still noisy as hell. I dial Faheem.

"Collect from Jaz."

"Hold on. I have a collect call from, what did you say, ma'am?"

"Jaz."

"From Jaz. Will you accept?"

Dial tone.

"Sorry, ma'am."

"No he fuckin' didn't!" I dial again. This time he won't even answer. I want to cry, but I can't look like no punk in here. I don't want to call my mom, so I call Kyra. Fine fuckin' time for Faheem to not be speaking to me.

"Collect from Jaz. Will you pay?"

"Jaz?" It's Marvin.

"Jaz. Will you pay, sir?"

"Yes, I will."

"Hey, Marvin."

"What's up, Jaz? You just missed Kyra. She went to school."

"I need a favor. I'm down here in the Mercer County Jail. I need you to call Faheem and tell him where I'm at."

"Damn, baby sis. You all right?"

"No. Tell Faheem I need a lawyer and to get me the fuck outta here. I also need somebody to get the key from Faheem and get my car. It's still parked at school."

"I'm on it, baby sis."

"Thanks, Marvin. I really appreciate it." I hang up. Fuck Faheem. He don't have to worry about me calling his black ass again.

"Jaz! Hey, Jaz!" I turn around to see Melissa. She is my brother Darien's "baby mama." She's a professional booster and paper hanger. "I thought that was you," she said, trying to squeeze me to death. "What the hell are you doing in here?"

"Wrong place, wrong time, girl. How you doing?" I can't tell her my business. She talk too much. I'll let her read it in the papers. I try to change the subject.

"How's my niece Myesha?" I asked her. She's talking, but I'm not listening. My mind is foggy. This is the last place I want to be.

"Jaz!" She's looking in my face.

"I'm listening." At least Melissa takes care of her daughter. She's just addicted to her hustle. I don't even ask her what she's in here for. She's still yapping.

"Melissa!" I try to shut her up. "I can't get the guard to give me shit. I need a washcloth, soap, toothbrush, comb. Look at me."

"Come on." She pulls my arm. "I'll get you hooked up." After about twenty minutes of haggling, she sure does get me hooked up. I have everything, even a new pair of panties and some shower shoes. I still feel like shit, though, and I'm hungry as hell.

By the time I shower, it's time to get in the lunch line. I can't believe what's supposed to be lunch. They give me a small metal cup with a metal spoon and tell me not to lose it. The cup has some watered down Kool-Aid in it. One gulp and it's gone. They give us a metal tray, divided into sections. One section holds four cold French fries, one holds a dried-up hot dog and the other has what I guess is chocolate pudding. I sure did take the free world for granted. I can't eat the hot dog, because no one's sure if it's pork or not. I do eat the four French fries, but I'm scared to eat the chocolate pudding. I walk over and sit down at the metal table and stool that are bolted down to the floor. Melissa is eating.

"Where's your hot dog?" she asks.

"It was hog, so I gave it away. Why, you wanted it?"

"Yeah."

"I hope you don't be feeding my niece that shit."

She shakes her head, but I know she's lying. That's one of the reasons I plan on building a boarding school. Bring these kids up right.

"Look over there," she tells me.

"Where?" I ask her, and she points to these two ugly, black, troll-looking, bulldaggin' twins.

"That's Marla and Darla," she says. "They head up the welcoming committee." One of them is playing with this Mexican girl's ponytail and the other one is picking up her food tray and metal cup, instructing the girl to come eat in their room. The girl gets up like a dummy and goes into their room. They cover up their cell with a blanket. After about an hour, the girl comes out looking like she seen a ghost. Melissa sees me staring at the girl and starts laughing.

"You're the newest kid on the block. They'll be coming after you next."

"Bullshit! Just make sure you don't let them jump me."

"I got your back."

"You better have it."

Just then about ten guards come running on the tier.

"Lockdown, ladies! To your cells!" They keep screaming it over and over.

"Something must have gone down with the men," Melissa says as she hurries toward her cell. I take that as a cue and hurry to mines. Now I know why the white crackhead was trying to start up a conversation. She's my cellmate. They keep us locked down until dinnertime. As soon as they crack the gates, I run to the phone.

"Shit!" All of them are turned off.

"Excuse me," I say to the guard. It isn't the same sister from this morning. This guard is ghetto fabulous. Long, flashy nails, crimped hair standing tall on top of her head, tight-ass uniform with plenty of cleavage.

"They'll be on shortly."

"When?"

"They'll be on shortly," she repeats.

"Jaz!" That's Melissa, calling me to get in line to get our dinner tray.

"When do you think they'll turn the phones on?" I'm desperate.

Melissa looks like she's almost six feet. She swings her ponytail back, looks down at me and says, "When they damned well feel like it."

I let out a sigh. We get our trays and sit down. It's the same watered-down Kool-Aid, a fish patty, carrots mixed with peas, two slices of white bread, what looks like mashed potatoes, and again that chocolate pudding. I'm starving. No sooner do I put some ketchup on my fish patty and dump the salt and pepper packets on my vegetables, that Melissa kicks me under the table.

"It's show time," she says.

The troll twins are coming our way. I ignore them and start to eat.

"What's your name?" The ugliest one says and begins running her hands through my hair.

"You have nice hair."

"Don't touch my hair," I tell her, still eating like a savage. She stops.

The ugly one picks up my tray.

"Come eat with us," she says. That must have given the other one courage, 'cause she starts back playing in my hair. I look at the one who's rubbing my hair and then I look at the one who's carrying my food. I'm still hungry as hell. I grab Melissa's tray and decide to go after the one with my food. I bang her over the head with all my strength. I keep hitting her like I'm in a frenzy. I hear clapping and whistling. Her twin sister doesn't even try to help her.

The next thing you know, I'm lifted clean up in the air and carried to my cell. They literally throw me inside. I bang my elbow against the stale toilet bowl. It seems like twenty or so guards are in there yelling, screaming bowl and locking every-one down. Since they don't have a hole for the women, they keep me locked in my cell. They don't even bother to do noth-ing to the ugly twins, and they don't bring me another tray of food. I'm pissed.

It's Friday, so that means I'm stuck in this dump for the entire weekend. They give me phone restriction as a punishment and I'm not able to take another shower until Sunday morning.

I'm in a depressed funk. I sleep and cry the whole weekend. I miss my bed. I miss Faheem. I miss everything that I took for granted. I try to figure out what Faheem probably said when he found out I was locked up for drugs. I'm pouring salt all over my wounds. I had been able to keep this hidden from Faheem for al-most two years, but after this, I might as well give up on us get-ting things back the way they were.

About 7:00 Monday morning, the guard with the ran-over shoes tells me to get all of my belongings.

"Am I being released?" My heart's pumping fast.

"I don't know. Where's your belongings?"

"I don't have anything."

They give me back my clothes and tell me to put them on. The clothes feel good. Then two brothers with U.S. Marshal jackets ask my name and some more questions, then handcuff my feet and wrists. They're real cordial, and make sure nothing is too tight. Now I'm in Federal custody.

"Where am I going now?" I ask them.

"To the Big Apple," says the one who looks like he's been partying all night.

The clock says 12:20 when we pull up to New York's MCC, Metropolitan Correctional Center. They transported me in a van. I got to listen to WBLS and they brought me some Burger King. I had to eat it with the handcuffs on, but I managed.

They put me inside a holding cell with a phone and unchained me. I was so thankful for that.

I call Marvin and Kyra collect again. Kyra gets all hysterical, wondering what I got myself into. After I finally convince her I'm all right and she calms down, she tells me that my bail was set at $200,000. That means we gotta come up with $20,000 in cash. She makes sure to tell me that Faheem is very pissed. He said he had no idea of what the fuck I was doing behind his back. He said he don't know what to expect next from me. He wants to know what other skeletons are going to come out the closet. That shit hurts me bad, him saying that.

But Kyra also tells me that Faheem did go pick up my car and parked it in front of the house. He got me a lawyer and gave Angel the $20,000 cash for my bail. Kyra says that my bail hearing is set for tomorrow and that I should be out by then. I'm so glad to hear that.

The Feds, from what I've seen, are much different than the county. The food is better, it's a little cleaner, and they even gave me a physical exam, which included a pregnancy test. And guess what? I'm pregnant. Five and a half weeks. When it rains, it pours. I thought that I was utterly depressed locked down in that cell all weekend, but when they tell me I'm pregnant, that's really depressing. I'm pregnant by a nigga who won't even talk to me. I'm in jail. I'm not finished with college yet. What else could go wrong?

Okay, for starters, it's now Tuesday, and I haven't been called to go to court. I'm feeling nauseous. I miss Faheem, but I refuse to call him. I don't want to talk to him over the phone. We gotta talk face-to-face. So I call Kyra again and she says that I will be out Wednesday.

Noon on Wednesday, they come and get me for my bail hearing and to read me my charges. Angel, Kyra, and Roz are sitting in the courtroom. I'm charged with "manufacturing meth with intent to distribute." Faheem gave my lawyer a $50,000 retainer, so of course he's very nice to me. When they release me, he tells me to be in his office first thing in the morning. He also says that I'm facing up to fifty years, and that Brett is already trying to negotiate a deal with the government.

When I get out front, my three friends are waiting for me. I burst out crying. Kyra is glowing, sporting her round belly. On the way home, I finally tell them I'm pregnant and that it don't look like me and Faheem will get things back the way they were. I tell them that a jail term is gonna put off me finishing school. They tell me that Marvin's birthday party is in two days. They think I should go, 'cause it would lighten me up. Plus, Faheem will be there. I tell them I'll be there, even though I'm scared shitless to face Faheem.

Chapter 27

When they pulled up in front of Jaz's house, the Escalade was parked out front. They dropped Jaz off and left. It was almost 6:00, and she was ecstatic to be home. She couldn't get over how good it felt to sit on her own toilet, to soak in a bathtub, and then lie in her own king-size bed, with clean sheets and a soft down comforter.

She was mentally drained and physically exhausted, so as soon as she finished eating, she went straight to bed, even though it was only 9:30. In the hours that she'd been home, she kept hoping Faheem would call. The only call she got was from her girls, checking up on her. By the time she went to bed, she knew Faheem wasn't gonna call and she decided that it was over between them.

She was at the lawyer's office the next morning by 9:00. Talking to him only made her hurt more. She took on this attitude: *Fuck it! You do the crime, be ready to do the time.* There was nothing she could do now to take back the mistakes she had made. She could only move forward.

After she left the lawyer's office, she went to the college to reschedule a couple of exams that she'd missed. Then she decided the rest of the day was all about her. First, she went to the Hyatt and ate a big lunch. Then she got a full body massage and mud wrap. She got a facial and got her feet and nails done. She went shopping and bought a black halter dress by Versace and some shoes to match. She picked up a silk Armani shirt for Marvin to thank him for helping her out. When she got home, she ate again, soaked in the tub and went to bed. She put the dead bolt on the door just in case Faheem decided to stop by.

The next morning Jaz stayed in the bed until 11:00. She took her time getting up and dressed, and didn't leave the house until it was time for her hair appointment at 4:00. Paul, her hairdresser, hooked her up, and that made her feel a little better. Afterward, she went home and ate again. The baby was giving her an appetite that she was not used to. She took a warm bath and soaked for almost an hour. Then she moisturized her skin and started getting dressed for Marvin's party. She didn't even know why she was going. If it wasn't for Kyra calling and leaving message after message on her machine, she probably would've stayed home. She didn't want Faheem to think that she was coming just to be begging and pleading with him.

Still, she did want to talk to Faheem. She knew she owed him an explanation for getting involved with this shit, especially after she was the one who made him stop selling when they first got together. Plus, she wanted to thank him for posting her bond and retaining a lawyer for her. She knew that only a nigga who got your back would do some shit like that. Faheem didn't hesitate coming to her aid, not even knowing what she had done. Faheem was definitely of a rare breed.

She put on her black Versace dress with the long split coming up the thigh. The dress showed plenty of cleavage, and she wore no bra. She checked herself in the mirror and could see that she had started to put on a few pounds. Even her breasts were getting rounder. She put on a beaded choker, with iced-up earrings to match. She slipped on her black Versace slingbacks, sprayed on some perfume, fingered her hair, grabbed her purse and Marvin's gift, and out the door she went.

"Kyra lives in the fuckin' boondocks!" Jaz cursed out loud in the car. She got lost and had to call Kyra for directions. By the time she got there, it was ten minutes to ten. Marvin had just finished cutting his cake.

There was a big crowd at the party. Jon B was squealing, "Alright Wit Me." The atmosphere was nice and Jaz smelled food. She was no longer nervous, because she hadn't seen Faheem's car out front. On the ride over she'd decided she didn't feel up to explaining anything to him tonight. She was glad he'd decided not to come.

She looked around and checked out all the fine brothers who was in the house. Obviously, from what was parked out front and all the Armani, Versace and ice flashing, they were some ballers. As she eased through the crowd looking for a familiar face, she noticed that Kyra had hired caterers and servers.

Jaz stopped at the beautifully laid buffet. At first she didn't know what to choose. She settled on cheese and crackers, strawberries and grapes. As she piled the food on her plate, she noticed a bunch of brothers in the room to her right. Most of them were smoking blunts, talking and laughing. Jaz scanned their faces and saw Marvin, a brother named Khalil, and then did a double take when she saw Faheem.

"Aw, damn!" she cursed under her breath. Faheem was puffing on a blunt and talking to two other brothers. She couldn't deny that the brother looked good. Her nipples got hard just from the sight of him. He wore a black Armani turtleneck sweater. That thing was defining all of his muscles. He had on the black leather pants that she had bought him.

Faheem glanced up and saw Jaz checking him out. She watched his eyes roam all over her body as he kept on talking. For a second she thought his eyes rested on her belly, which had started to swell a tiny bit. Then some female with a long weave and a sequined mini-dress tapped on the door and called his name. Jaz turned away and went to find Kyra.

She found Kyra and Angel upstairs. Angel was wrapping Marvin's gift.

"Always at the last minute, huh, Angel?"

Angel and Kyra looked up at her and started laughing.

"Shut up!" Angel joked.

"How long have you been here?" Kyra asked, giving her a hug.

"About a half hour. The place looks real nice. Y'all got it goin' on!"

"Thanks. I'll be glad when it's over. I'm beat. How are you?"

"I was fine until I saw Faheem."

"I'm sure you was. I know you noticed that he didn't come alone," Angel said.

"Yeah, I saw her. The bitch do look good. I have to give her that."

"What'chu gonna do?" Kyra asked.

"I'm not sure yet."

"Shit. You better go get your man!" Angel yelped.

"You didn't even tell him you was pregnant, did you?"

"No, Kyra. I didn't."

"Like I said. Go get your man. Don't be stupid, Jaz. That nigga is good to you. Or would you rather have a scrub-ass, lying, can't-fuck ho?"

"Fuck you, Angel."

"I rest my case. Go get your man, Jaz. You the one started all this shit in the first place."

They didn't have to tell her twice. Jaz left the room and headed downstairs. She stopped on the stairs and scanned the room in search of Faheem. When she spotted him, he was talking with the female with the long weave and sequined mini-dress.

"Fuck it!" Jaz said as she approached Faheem. She had nothing to lose, so she was going for what she knew.

Just as she got a few feet away from Faheem, her ex, Sabu, grabbed her. Sabu was a tall, dark and very handsome baller.

"Come here, Jaz!" He hugged her and kissed her neck. "What's up, baby?"

"How you doing, Sabu?" she asked him, looking to Faheem out the corner of her eye. He was staring at them.

"Damn, you smell good, baby." Sabu inhaled her perfume. "Why'd you leave me for that nigga Faheem?"

"Sabu, don't even try it."

"I'm serious, Jaz. You never said shit." He kissed her on the cheek, then slid his hand down on her ass. "Didn't I used to make you climb the walls?" He kissed her cheek again. "Damn. I miss that shit!"

"Yeah, you used to. But Faheem makes me climb the walls, the ceiling and the roof."

"Jaz, you know I'm still crazy about you. Let me take you out tonight."

"Sabu, I got a man to take me out."

"I can't tell, baby. I ain't no hater, but your man didn't come here alone tonight. He left you to come here all by yourself? I would never leave your fine ass by yourself."

"I know my memory is right, and I remember that you had *no problems* leaving me by myself. You used to leave your garden unattended. That's why Faheem came home and took over."

"Yeah. I have to admit I was wrong for that shit. Like I said, though, the nigga ain't over here."

"If you don't get your hand off my ass and your lips off my neck, he will be over here."

"Well, I'll tell you what. If he don't come over here in the next three minutes, you going home with me. If he do, well, I'll give the nigga his space."

That shit sounded good to Jaz. She was thinking about how she hadn't been fucked in almost two months. At least she knew Sabu. He wasn't shit, and he definitely couldn't lay it down like Faheem. But he'd do for one night. Then she remembered how he could never get it right when he was giving head and decided not to waste her time. Besides, Sabu was a lying ho. That's why she left him in the first place. Just as she was about to tell him forget it and slap his hand off her ass, Faheem yelled.

"Sabu!"

"Oh, shit!" Jaz mumbled.

Sabu looked up and started backing away from Jaz.

"What up, Faheem?" he asked as he crossed his hands in front of himself to hide his already hard dick.

"What's the matter with you, man? Why the fuck you all up on mines, son?" Faheem was talking loud.

Sabu raised his hands up in the air. "No disrespect, man. I thought wasn't nothing up, man."

They both stood there, staring each other down. Faheem grabbed Jaz's hand and pulled her to him.

"So what's up?" he asked her.

"That depends on you, Faheem." She looked him in the eye. He leaned over and kissed her. His tongue roamed around her mouth and his hands wandered all over her ass. Jaz could hardly breathe, but it felt so good. She knew this was where she wanted to be forever.

Faheem went to kiss her neck, but stopped to glare at Sabu. "You smell like this nigga. Go wash that shit off and meet me in that office back there, next to the kitchen. We gotta straighten some shit out."

When she came into the office, he was leaning up against one of the desks with his arms folded.

"Close the door," he told her. She closed it and sat down in a recliner. "Tell me about this shit that you got locked up for."

Jaz told him everything. From the first day two years ago when she hooked up with Brett to how much she was getting paid. From her lying to him that Mondays and Thursdays she had late classes, to the raid, to her incident in jail. When she finished, she was crying.

"Those are some big-ass skeletons, Jaz. You didn't trust me enough to tell me this? You been sneaking around for two fucking years."

"I'm sorry, Faheem. I figured it would be better that way." She kept crying.

"Better for who, Jaz?" She didn't answer. "Damn!" He handed her some tissue. "I can't get over this shit. You sure had me fuckin' fooled. So, tell me this. Did you fuck that nigga you had up in my crib?"

"Fuck you, Faheem! You know I didn't." She stared at him as she wiped her tears. "You've been treating me like I'm guilty of fuckin' somebody, and I'm not. I'm tired of you treating me like this. I made a mistake. It was a big fuckin' mistake, Faheem. So fuck you. I'm tired. You've been fuckin' draining my energy. I love you, Faheem, and I would never dog you like that, but I'm tired. I can't put up with this bullshit no more."

Somebody knocked on the door. Neither of them moved. They knocked again. Jaz got up and opened it.

"Is Faheem in here?" It was the female who Faheem brought to the party.

"What the fuck do you want?" Jaz screamed.

"'Scuze me?"

Jaz turned to Faheem. "Faheem, tell this bitch that you got a woman, that she's pregnant, and she's living in your house. Then tell this bitch she's only been a fuck for the past, however long you been fuckin' her."

"You just told her, loud and clear." Faheem laughed. Jaz slammed the door in her face and locked it.

"Faheem, you got me so fuckin' riled up I could kill you."

"So, you're pregnant?"

Jaz stopped ranting and nodded her head slowly.

"Come here." He held out his arms. She went to him, and he wrapped them around her. She started crying. "I'm sorry, baby," he kept whispering as he rocked her back and forth.

"I've been so stressed, and you've been the main cause of it."

"I'm sorry, baby. I didn't know. You keep shit from me, Jaz. That ain't right. You know I got your back, regardless. We can't keep shit from each other."

"How long you been fuckin' that girl?"

"I didn't."

"You lie."

"I swear on my grandfather. I was thinking about it, though."

"You full of it, Faheem."

"Can't I have a kiss?"

"Nope."

"How come?"

"Now I'm mad."

"You let that nigga Sabu kiss you."

"He kissed me on my neck. I didn't kiss him."

"How far are we?"

"We?"

"Yeah, we."

"Six weeks."

"That's why your ass feel rounder. And look at your tits. They're rounder, too." He started massaging them. "Can we start over?"

"If you want to."

"Forgive each other, no lying and hidin' shit?"

She wiped her tears and nodded.

"Can I have a kiss now?" he asked.

She kissed him softly on his lips and wrapped her arms around his neck.

"I've missed you a lot," he whispered in her ear.

"I bet I've missed you more," she told him. They kissed passionately and didn't let go for almost ten minutes. She kept her arms around his neck and he slid his hands up under her dress, grabbed her ass and started grinding nice and slow. She could feel him getting a hard-on.

"Faheem, baby, let's go home."

He ignored her and slid her halter top to the side. He licked and sucked her nipples.

"Come on, Faheem. Let's go."

"Okay, we'll go in a minute." He lifted her up, set her on top of the desk and slid his hand between her legs. He maneuvered her thong off and put two fingers deep inside her. He massaged her clit with his thumb.

"Faheem, baby, that feels so good," she moaned, "but not here." He started flicking his fingers over her clit faster and faster, until she started shaking and trembling and came all over his hand. He grabbed the box of tissue and wiped off his hand. He kissed her, then pulled out his dick.

"Faheem, not here. This is disrespectful."

"This ain't no church, baby. The door is locked. Ten more

minutes, Jaz. Look how hard my dick is. What am I supposed to do?"

"If you would have stopped when I told you to, it wouldn't be hard."

"Ten minutes, baby." He didn't wait for an answer. He put one of her legs around his waist and the other in the crook of his arm then slid his dick inside her. She let out a loud moan.

"Damn, baby. Your pussy is hot and juicy."

"See what you've been missing," she whispered. "Now apologize and promise me you'll never leave me again," she said as she gripped his dick with her muscles.

"I'm so sorry, baby. I love you, baby. I'll never leave you." He quickened up his pace. "Go ahead, baby," he told her. "Get your shit off. I can't hold out much longer."

Jaz held on tighter, positioned herself to get just the right amount of friction on her clit, and after about a few more strokes she was having an orgasm that came in bigger and bigger waves. Faheem emptied himself inside her.

"That felt so good, baby." He ran his tongue over her neck. "Now we can go home."

When they got to the house, Faheem made sweet, sweet love to Jaz all night. He kept kissing and rubbing her stomach, telling her not to worry about anything. He would always take care of his.

Chapter 28

Faheem's pager kept going off. Jaz looked at the digital clock. It was 5:49. The pager vibrated again, making noise on the nightstand.

"Faheem, answer that pager or turn it off, baby." It buzzed again. "Faheem!" She shook him. "Get your pager."

Faheem felt on the nightstand, knocking over a glass and a picture frame. He picked it up, hit the light and checked the number. He threw the pager back on the nightstand. It buzzed again.

"Faheem, who is that blowing up your pager this early in the morning? Why didn't you turn it off?"

"Don't know, baby. Call 'em for me." He pulled the sheet over his head.

Jaz climbed over him and snatched the pager up. She went through the numbers and saw that same number was in there about ten times. She picked up the phone and dialed the number.

"Hello," the female voice said.

"Who is paging Faheem?"

"This is Trina. Who is this?"

"This is his woman. Why the fuck you blowin' up my man's pager at six in the morning?"

"Let me speak to Faheem."

"Like I said, ho, Faheem got a woman, so find somebody else to page. Faheem! Tell this ho to stop paging you," she yelled and threw the phone at him.

"Baby, what's the matter with you?" He pulled the sheet off his head.

"Tell that bitch that you got a woman and to stop blowin' up your fuckin' pager!"

"Why you wake me up for this shit?" Faheem snatched the phone up. "Who the fuck is this? Trina. How the fuck you get my pager number? Naw, baby, it ain't that kind of party no more and don't tell me you ain't know that shit either." He threw the phone back at Jaz. "Why you wake me up for that bullshit?"

Jaz hung up the phone. "Don't start no shit, Faheem." She turned her back to him.

"Oh, so you jealous now?" He smirked, wrapping his arms and legs around her, and then biting her cheek.

"Stop playing, Faheem."

"Baby, you know it's all about you and my baby, so don't even trip." He kissed her on the neck and they went back to sleep.

Later on that morning the phone started ringing.

"Jaz, get the phone," Faheem said, half asleep.

"What?"

"Answer the phone, baby."

Jaz checked the clock. 8:12. "Hello?"

It was Micki, and she was crying. Jaz turned over on her back and stared up at the ceiling.

"Jaz, I can't take it here with Grandma. She's driving me crazy. I gotta get my own place. Can you help me out?"

"I can help you out, but Micki, you only working part-time.

What's gonna happen when the first month's rent is due? What about Brian? Didn't he want you to move in with him?"

"I'm grown, Jaz. I can handle paying rent. I gotta get the fuck outta here. Fuck Brian! I'm not feeling him."

"Put Grandma on the phone, Micki. Let me speak to her." Their grandmother got on the phone, yelling. "Is this Jasmine?"

"Yes, ma'am, it's me."

"Micki is back using that shit again. She's gonna get me put out, and she gonna end up back behind bars. I keep try'na tell her, but she won't listen. She needs to go, but them children need to stay here."

"Grandma, she ain't using drugs. I wish y'all would stop fightin'. I'm gonna help her get her own place. Can you get along for a week or two more?"

"She can't handle her own place if she using them drugs. Don't waste your money." Jaz heard Micki arguing at her Grandma in the background.

"All right, Grandma. I'll come and see y'all later on."

"Bye, baby."

"Shit!" Jaz slammed down the phone.

Faheem rolled over, lifted her negligee and began kissing her stomach. He raised his head up and looked at her. "What's the matter?"

"I gotta help Micki get a place. She and my grandma is about to kill each other."

"I don't want you stressing about shit. I'll get somebody to find her a place." Jaz didn't say anything. "Did you hear me?"

"I hear you."

"I'm here for you, baby." He wrapped her in his arms and held her until she fell back to sleep.

Chapter 29

Jaz had another appointment with her lawyer. He told her that there were seventeen other people arrested in connection with the case. They were distributing the meth that she and Brett had been cooking up. Luckily for her, none of those people knew about her. But Brett knew, and he was ready to make a deal with the government. They were planning on pinning kingpin charges on Jaz. Brett's testimony, along with $12,000.00 cash and the supplies that were found at the house, were the evidence that they had against her. Jaz would be fighting a fifty-year-to-life sentence. She didn't hold out much hope for her freedom by the time she was through at the lawyer's office. At least until she found out about Brett's fate.

A week after Jaz met with the lawyer, Brett Dumont was found dead at the steering wheel of his car. They removed twenty-seven bullets from his body before his family could bury him.

With the government's star witness gone, Jaz's charges were downgraded to "conspiracy to manufacture with intent to distribute a controlled substance." They offered her a plea bargain of eleven years. She declined. Leaving the government no choice but to go to trial.

"Faheem, did you smoke Brett?" Jaz asked when they were alone one day.

"What?"

"Did you smoke Brett?"

"What kind of question is that?" He twisted the cap off the bottled water and took a long gulp. "You know them white boys be into all types of shit."

"Faheem, baby," Jaz asked with tears rolling down her face. "I won't be able to handle it if we're both sitting in prison."

"Jaz." He massaged her shoulders. "I told you I don't want you stressing, baby. Why can't you do like I'm telling you? Stop sweating the little shit." He hugged her. "Let me do all the sweatin'. Worry about your finals. You got two more exams and the semester will be over, right?"

"Yeah."

"Well, worry about acing those, okay?" He kissed her on the lips, grabbed his keys and left.

Jaz couldn't help but stress these days. Not only was she worried about her case, but her grandmother and Micki were still arguing all the time. Grandma Rachel kept accusing Micki of selling crack out of her house. Jaz knew that Micki wasn't using again and she was glad of that. Micki was taking good care of the children and was able to get a job full time at the DMV. The only drugs she was taking were prescription pills for her depression. Still, she had to get out of Grandma's house, so Faheem found her and the kids a place in his building. It wouldn't be vacant for another couple of weeks, so Jaz was dealing with the arguments from both sides until then.

A few days later, Jaz was still stressed. She hadn't seen Faheem since he'd grabbed his keys and left the other day, though he did manage to stop by her lawyer's office and give him another thirty grand. That got the lawyer up off his fat ass, and he got the plea bargain down to five years. They said all she had to do was plead guilty to "conspiracy to travel in interstate commerce in order to possess with intent to distribute, a Schedule II controlled substance." Jaz considered the offer, but told the lawyer she didn't want to do no time since she had a baby on the way. He told her that he was working on it.

Jaz was thinking about the possibility of prison as she removed two bags of groceries from the back of her Escalade. She trucked them up the stairs to Faheem's apartment. Even though he spent most of his nights at the house, he spent his days here when he wasn't at one of his liquor stores. Since she hadn't seen him for a few days, Jaz had decided to come by and fix a dinner at his place, hoping he'd come home soon.

She got ready to put her key in the door when it opened up. Three dudes came out, each one carrying two suitcases. One of them she recognized as Buju, from the club. None of them spoke to Jaz. They went briskly past her. As Jaz went inside and carried the grocery bags to the kitchen, they came back in to get the last of the suitcases. Buju stayed behind to talk to Faheem, who also hadn't said anything to Jaz yet. She could tell it was all business up in here. She kept herself busy in the kitchen, putting away the food and loading the dishwasher until she heard Faheem walk Buju to the door and tell him good-bye. Jaz went into the living room.

"Hey, baby," he said as he picked up two briefcases and headed to the spare bedroom where the safe was.

"Faheem," she called after him. "Is that why I haven't seen you in three days? You been hustling?"

"Wait a minute, baby. I'll be right there."

She didn't wait. She went right back to the bedroom where he was hunched over the safe.

"Faheem, you have four liquor stores and four check cashing

places, you got a stash and I have a stash. Why are you still hust-ling?"

"That was it," he told her as he stood to face her. "I'm finished Jaz, I told you I want to be retired when I turn thirty-five. I got a baby on the way. I got to pay them slimy-ass lawyers. We need a cushion. I just had that one run. You know you don't want no broke-ass nigga." He stopped himself and came close to her. "You don't need to know any of this. Baby, I told you to let me do all the worrying."

"Faheem, you're taking too many chances. I know you had something to do with Brett, and now you're making runs. With both of us in prison, having a cushion ain't gonna do us no good. We won't be able to spend it. They giving out fuckin' life sentences like they going out of style. We go to jail, we lose everything. Even the baby." She burst out crying.

"Trust me, baby." He grabbed her. "I'm through. I'm not in jail. You're not in jail. What's wrong with you?"

"You really want to know?"

"Yeah, I do."

"I'm scared. I'm mad at you. I'm mad at myself. I'm stressed. Since I've been pregnant I've been on an emotional roller coaster. I miss you. Do you want me to continue?"

"I love you, Jaz, and I'll always have your back. You should know that by now." He kissed her.

"I know that, Faheem. I'm just saying it would be fucked up if we both went to prison. And, I can't be mad with nobody but myself."

"You got me worried. You're gonna have a nervous breakdown if you don't stop. If something happens to my baby, Jaz, I'm gonna lose it. Then, you'll have something to worry about. And you're gonna be kicking yourself in the butt. You need to relax. Let me run you some bath water."

He filled the tub with steaming water and jasmine-scented bubbles. He took off her clothes for her and put her in the tub. He sat beside the tub and sponged her down as he tried to get her to relax a little. When she got out the tub, he dried her off and oiled down her entire body. Then he gave her a full body massage until she was finally relaxed and began smiling.

"You want to go away this weekend?" he asked her.

"That would be nice."

"You feel any better?" he asked as he stroked the hair between her legs.

"One hundred percent better. Thank you, Faheem. You are so good to me. You know you the shit, right?"

"Yeah, I know." He inserted one finger into her pussy and started gently probing her. "I can't believe that three days have passed since I got me some of this."

"You slippin', Faheem."

"I'm getting ready to make up for it. Look how hard my dick is." He lay on his back. "Get on top, baby. I want to see how much you miss me."

"This is how I got pregnant in the first place. Missing you and gettin' on top." She eased down on his dick and started grinding nice and slow. Jaz let out a soft moan and they moved together, slow and sweet.

"I love you, Faheem."

"Are you ready to be my wife?" he asked her, then started caressing her nipples with his tongue.

"Oooh, Faheem, don't make me come yet," she moaned. It was too late. Jaz's breathing started getting heavier. She held him tight and pressed her hips into him. She kept repeating his name like it was music.

"Let it go, baby," he told her as her clit pressed against him faster. Finally she let it go, screaming his name one more time. She held him tight, still trembling after she was done.

"Baby, answer my question. You ready to be my wife?"

"Yeah, baby, I am."

Faheem held her close and caressed her growing stomach. His dick was getting hard, but just as he got ready to slide up in there again, the phone rang.

"Damn!" he groaned. He had been expecting a business call.

"Don't answer it, baby." She ran her tongue over his nipples.

"I have to. I'm expecting a call at 10:00." He picked up the phone and rolled away from Jaz. "What up?" He picked his half a blunt out of the ashtray and lit it. "For when? . . . What time . . . Naw. No can do, man!"

Jaz rolled over and started kissing him on his stomach. He ran his fingers through her hair.

Kiss me! he mouthed while listening on the phone. She gave him a sloppy kiss, pulling on his bottom lip. Then she grabbed his dick.

"I'm not sure, man. How long? . . . Uh-huh." She put his dick in her mouth. "Dayum, baby!" he said to Jaz. "Yeah, I'm still here," he said into the phone. "Anything else? Okay, man. I'm out. Peace!"

He put down the receiver. "Shit, Jaz. This fuckin' feels good!" He grabbed her head and held on tight. He closed his eyes and tried to push his dick in as far as he could.

"Oh, shit, Jaz." He came hard. "God damn, baby. That was some good head. Who you been practicing on?"

"Fuck you, Faheem!" She got up.

"You know I'm playin'. Come here. Don't get up!"

"I wanna take a shower."

"Give me a kiss first." She crawled in between his legs and he put his tongue deep into her mouth. The phone rang again.

"Damn! Can't get no privacy." He stuck two fingers inside her.

"Answer the phone, Faheem."

"You the one who said let it ring." He pulled his fingers out of her pussy and ran his tongue all around them. Jaz sat up and answered the phone.

"Hello?"

Faheem spread her thighs, then leaned over and put his tongue in as deep as it would go. He brought it out and circled her clit while she talked.

"I'm fine, Tommy." Her voice was trembling a little as she arched her back. "I'll get him. Hold on." She placed the phone down on the bed. "Hurry baby, it's for you." She grabbed his head. "That feels good, baby. Faster, baby. That's it. Oh, Fahe . . ." She came again. Faheem kissed her, then picked up the phone.

"Who dis? . . . Why you had to call now, man? This shit could have waited." He watched Jaz get up and go toward the shower. "Hold on, man. I got another call." He clicked over. "What up? Oh, hey, Angel. She in the shower . . . You can't wait? What's so important? A'ight, hold on." He clicked back over to Tommy.

"I gotta go, man." Then he clicked back to Angel.

"Angel. What happened? . . . Damn! Do Brian know? . . . God damn! . . . Hell, no. I can't tell her this shit. Was she that fuckin' depressed? . . . This is going to fuck her up. I can't tell her this shit . . . I'm out. Peace." He lay back on his pillow and worried about how Angel's news was gonna hurt Jaz.

Jaz finally came out the bathroom. "Dry me off, Faheem." She threw him the towel. "You are the shit. I can't be mad at them hos for sweatin' you."

He grabbed her and hugged her real hard.

"I can't breathe, Faheem. What's the matter with you?"

"Baby, I got some bad news." He kissed her forehead.

"What? What, Faheem? What happened?"

She started shaking. "Is it my mother?"

"No, baby. It's your sister. Micki."

"Oh, God. What she do, Faheem? Tell me what she did!" she screamed.

"She took the three girls up to the fourteenth floor of your grandmother's building and made them all jump. All four of them are dead. I'm sorry, baby."

Jaz fainted. When she woke up, she was in the maternity ward at the hospital. She had a monitor on her stomach, checking the baby's heartbeat, and an IV stuck in her arm. She remained in there for almost two weeks. They wanted to keep an eye on her and the baby, since everyone was so worried about her mental state after the death of her sister and the kids.

Faheem was able to get them to postpone her trial for six more weeks. Jaz wasn't holding up well. The doctors didn't even allow her to go to the funeral. They said it would have been too much for her. Faheem hired her a couple of nurses to stay with her during the day.

When the trial finally started, Jaz was five months pregnant. Kyra was nine months, ready to have her baby any time. The trial lasted for two weeks. The so-called jury of her peers found Jasmine Denise Taylor guilty on all counts. She was sentenced to seventeen years in Federal custody.

THUGS AND THE WOMEN WHO LOVE THEM

WAHIDA CLARK

ABOUT THIS GUIDE

The suggested questions are intended to enhance
your group's reading of this book.

DISCUSSION QUESTIONS

1. Should Angel, a law student, be involved with Snake, a pimp?

2. Could Snake love Angel? Do you think he is serious about quitting the pimp game and settling down with her?

3. What do you have to say about Angel's side hustle of writing checks? Is it hypocritical? Survival? Greed?

4. Can a 14-year-old, like Kyra, and 22-year-old Marvin be soul mates?

5. Are you angry at Marvin for getting her strung out on dope? Or does Kyra get the blame?

6. Is Kyra using Tyler?

7. What should Kyra have done when Marvin knocked on her door?

8. What kind of man is Faheem?

9. Was Jaz's inviting Smooth over to Faheem's house an innocent mistake?

10. Jaz refused to start a relationship with Faheem until he quit the drug game. She began making drugs/meth. Is she hypocritical or was it survival?

11. Which couple do you think has the most promise? Why do you think so?

Up Close and Personal with Wahida Clark. Author of the
Essence **bestseller**
Thugs and the Women Who Love Them.

What is the book about?
- Ghetto/street life, it's reality fiction. The underground reading population seems to have an insatiable appetite for it.

What messages are you hoping to portray?
- Even though it's reality fiction, for now I write to entertain and to make a living. When I have money, I'll write to uplift.

Are you still incarcerated? Why were you incarcerated?
- Yes, I'm still on lock. My charges are conspiracy/money laundering, mail and wire fraud. My sentence is 125 months, that's 10½ years.

Where do you call home?
- New Jersey. Trenton to be exact. I had moved to the ATL and kicked it down there for four years. That's where I caught my case. I loved it down there. Looking forward to going back.

Was your upbringing average?
- What's average? I came up in the hood and you know how that is. Survival of the fittest, welfare, food stamps, government cheese, weed, boosting, partying. I had the average dysfunctional family (smile). I always had a roof over my head and clothes on my back. A single parent home in the projects, Donnelly Homes, until I was about nine or ten, then we moved to the West Side of town with my Aunt Ann and Uncle John. May he rest in peace. That was all love.

Who or what inspired you to be a writer?

• Who? My family. I'm a provider. What? The future. I'm confined but racking my brain trying to figure out how I can eat the day that I hit the bricks. I refuse to put myself in the situation when on that day, I'm trying to figure out how me and mines is gonna eat. That has to be already covered. So, my job at the time was prison librarian. And on days when we were short of help I would have to be there at 8 a.m. And nine times out of ten, I'd be in there all by myself. I would use that time to get caught up on my letter writing, magazine and book reading. In the magazines I would see the black authors and I would read their interviews. I told myself, "I can do that." They would mention their struggles and I could relate.

Then I would look around at all the books on the shelves, admire the titles and the authors' names and would visualize my name on the spine of a book on a bookshelf. That's when it clicked. I decided that I would become a writer. I said its legal, its something that I can do and do now! Shortly afterward, a lady who used to be a literary agent (who was also an inmate where I was) had volunteered to give a Creative Writing Course. And the rest is history. It's something how when you put those thoughts out there, the Universe takes over.

Why did you choose Thugs and the Women Who Love Them to write about?

• Actually, the story was originally supposed to be about four girls from the hood who vowed not to become victims of their environment. I wanted to show that they were strong and how they overcame hard trials and kept on striving. But as I kept writing, each of the female characters took on a life of her own, but it turned into *Thugs and the Women Who Love Them* in which the male characters sort of took over.

Snake was off the chain! What's up with that?

• (Laughs) That style or mode of writing was my paying tribute to the trailblazers of ghetto fiction; Donald Goines, Iceberg Slim, Nathan 'Booby' Herd.

How do you feel about being in prison and writing such a powerful book?

• I'm glad it's considered powerful (smile). As far as being in prison and writing a book: a sista had to do what a sista had to do! It wasn't something that I actually planned to do, so that makes me feel good. And writing a hot novel while on lock makes it feel that much better. Especially when I get letters from brothas and sistas in my situation who say that I inspired them. Now, that's what's up!

Have there been many obstacles to overcome?

• With any new venture there are always gonna be obstacles. We should welcome obstacles. They are one of the things that make the great great, when we can overcome them to succeed. The great ones never make excuses as to why something can't be done. Plus, I am blessed to have a wonderful team outside of these walls that allowed me to reach my goals much sooner than I could have without them. I have a very good team. I'm blessed.

Are there any beefs in the writing game similar to those in the music industry?

• It's crazy, but yeah I've heard of several of which I have no understanding. Just because a reader is a fan of mine and buys my book, in no way does it mean that the same reader won't go buy another author's book. That's ridiculous. There are too many good books out there to read, and like I mentioned earlier, the reader's appetite is insatiable. Us authors can't get our books out fast enough to satisfy their appetites. And that's a good thing. There is enough money out there for all of us. You feel me? I recall teasing an author, telling him since he blew up he can't write a sista no more. He said you down with the enemy, referring to another author. All I could do was laugh. Unbelievable! I said I'm in prison. I know you're not threatened. I'm a fan of yours!

Do you have future projects coming our way?
• Definitely. There is my third project that's FIRE, called *Payback Is a Mutha*. Then my fourth joint, is a short story called "Enemy in My Bed." And I got Part III to my Thug series, the book after the sequel *Every Thug Needs a Lady!* Everybody's dying (hint, hint) to know what happens to Snake, Trae and Kaylin. You know I like to keep my peeps hangin', anticipatin' and feenin' for my next joint. The title is *Payback Is a Mutha* was originally called *Don't Knock Tha' Hustle* but someone else got that title.

Do you think one or more of your books may end up on the screen and stage?
• Oh, fo' sho'! That's one of my goals. I would like Roc-A-Fella Films to holla at a sista as well as a few others. You know who you are!

Are you coming home soon?
• I'm presently waiting for an answer from my 2255 motion. I took my case to trial and lost. That's right. This sista here lives by the code: Death before dishonor. However, I lost two appeals and worse case scenario, I can't hit the bricks until '07. But I'm claiming '05 especially with these new Supreme Court decisions *Blakely vs. Washington* and *Booker & FanFan*.

I take it that you don't have no love for snitches?

• Not at all. When everything is good, they eatin', ballin', bills are getting paid, they are taking care of their families, it's all gravy and they are happy to play their part. But as soon as the shit hits the fan their weakness and hypocrisy gets put on blast. The sad thing is without snitches the government ninety-eight percent of the time doesn't have a case. Snitches tell shit that the government wasn't even aware of. If everyone on my case would have stood tall, we all would have walked.

What were you into before you were incarcerated?

• Running my businesses and working. Ironically, working is how I caught my case.

Has your time in prison affected your views on life?

• Definitely. I appreciate being with and having a family that much more. I no longer take the simple things in life for granted. Freedom. My physical freedom is truly valued. If you have been locked down or did time with a loved one, you understand what I'm saying.

I heard you hung out with Martha Stewart. What is she like?

• I didn't hang out with her. I met with her on several occasions in an attempt to put together a business seminar, with her allowing us to pick her brain. And I met with her to go over my business plan for my publishing company. She gave me some very valuable feedback. Martha is cool. She did her little five months like a trooper and was always willing to help you out if she could. Plus, my agent used to date her niece and told Martha to look me up when she got here. Which she did. The first day she hit the compound she was asking who knows Wahida Clark. By that evening I had got the message, and I went to meet her. I thought she was going to be standoffish. But, to my surprise, she was the total opposite.

How did the inmates treat her? Were they hatin'?

• Like I said, I didn't hang with her. Whenever I got with her it was always on a business tip. So I didn't always see how the rest of the population was treating her. You always gonna have your haters and I would hear different comments. But me? I'm not a hater. I'm a congratulator. I'm trying to get where she is. She is big time. Certified gangster for real. Whenever you can do time and turn on the preview channel and see your TV show getting ready to air: that's big! Whenever you can do time and your magazine is coming out every month: that's big! Whenever you can do time and two major retail chains carry your products, merge and you make a billion: that's big! Whenever you can do time and your stock from your company is steadily rising: that's big! Whenever you can do time and when you set your foot out the gate a TV show is waiting for you: that's big! Whenever you can do time and bounce on your own private jet: that's big! I'm sure you get my point. I think she's a brilliant businesswoman.

Do you believe in God? If so, has your belief played a major role in your writing career?

• My God is Allah, the Supreme Being. I asked him to bless and to guide me to write tha bomb book. He answers all of my prayers. In time and on time.

So, you're Muslim. Who do you follow?

• Yes, I am Muslim. I don't advocate many different kinds. There is only one Muslim: the one who submits with all his heart and soul to Allah and Muhammad.

How old are you?
- I'm ageless.

You can write Wahida at Wahida Clark, P.O. Box 8520, Newark, NJ 07108.

The following are sample chapters from Wahida Clark's
highly anticipated upcoming novel
PAYBACK IS A MUTHA.
This book will be available in April 2006
wherever books are sold.
ENJOY!

Chapter 1

SHAN AND BRIANNA

"Gurrll, guess what?" Shan was almost jumping up and down as she shouted at her best friend, Brianna, through the phone.

"Why are you screaming?" Brianna asked with obvious agitation.

"I got the job, girl! I got the J, mutha-fuckin' O, B!"

"Which one? You done interviewed with damn near fifty thousand people."

"The computer instructor for the prison. They just hung up."

Brianna sucked her teeth and rolled her eyes. "It took them long enough. I would have changed my mind. I don't see why you want to work for the prison system or work, period! All these niggas out here with money."

"Bitch, please! Everybody ain't a gold diggin' ho like you. I need my own cash and I don't want to suck dicks to get it!"

"You better get with the program. That's why your broke ass got two niggas and you can't even pay your bills now."

"Bitch, just because you was in prison and I choose to work for the prison, don't hate. Congratulate! Plus, I've only been kickin' it with Calvin for a month. He likes me because he sees it ain't all about the cash with me. I'd rather get my own and have my own."

"Please! Do you hear yourself? Like I said, you better step up your game and get with the program. You can fall for that weak shit if you want. That nigga knows it's all about the cash. Niggas ain't nothin' but tricks."

"Do you, B, 'cause you know I'ma do me, so are you down to help me celebrate or what?"

"Like I said, if you were on top of your game . . ."

"Girl," Shan interrupted, "I bet you even hustle niggas in your sleep! Don't you?"

They both burst out laughing. Brianna knew for sure that Shan was telling the truth. "Let me make a few phone calls and I'll call you around nine. Dress to impress. You know I gotta kill two birds with one stone. I'ma celebrate with you and see who I can get with later," Brianna said.

"Yeah I know how you do. But don't worry about me dressing to impress. You just make sure you are here by nine. Don't call at nine. Be here at nine! Peace out."

"Wait. What are you getting ready to do?" Brianna asked.

"Take a beauty nap. What you think?"

"Whatever, ho. Do you."

"I'm trying. Peace."

After Brianna hung up the phone with Shan she headed for the bathroom. She stood in front of the mirror as she pinned up her $1,200.00 weave. "Where should we go tonight?" She asked the mirror. It was Friday night, and she wanted to take full advantage of it. Her girl, Shan, loved the hip-hop clubs, but B's first preference was anything where the *real* ballers hung, so she knew she had to choose the spot.

She and Shan had been friends since the third grade. Everyone thought that they were family. Shan was closer to Brianna than her own blood sister. Unforeseen forces bound them close together like when Shan's parents were killed in that fatal car accident, and when Brianna got pregnant in the seventh grade and her mother put her out. They really leaned on one another. Even though Brianna lost her baby, her mother still wouldn't take her back. When social services came and took Peanut and Shan away, that left Brianna homeless. When a relative came and rescued them from the group home, that's when Brianna was taken off the streets. They made sure Brianna came with them. But her mother didn't allow her back home until she went to tenth grade.

The two friends were night and day in just about every way. Brianna was tall and Shan was short. Brianna had to wear Gucci, Prada and Chanel while Shan preferred Sean John, Baby Phat and FUBU. Brianna had the weave, fake nails and a boob job while Shan had the locks, sported her real nails and refused to do the makeup thing. Brianna went to prison while Shan now chose to work at a prison. Brianna lived large off the ballers while Shan preferred the legit businessman or blue collar worker. Which is why everyone couldn't figure out how they remained so close over the years.

During Brianna's eighteen-month prison bid the only two people who stuck by her was Shan and one of her sugar daddys by the name of Nick. He kept money on her books and allowed her to run up his phone bill. She had mad love for Nick, but she had been out now for a little over a year and he felt like she still owed him. Brianna had recently told him that she gave him enough pussy to consider her debt paid in full.

Upon hearing the phone ring, Brianna snatched it up. "Hello."

"What up, B?"

"You."

"You don't even know who this is."

"Oh, I know who this is." She teased. "There is only one Shadee."

"Act like you know, girl! I thought I was gonna have to tap that ass. I need to swing by later on."

"Around what time? Me and my girl is going out. Can you come before six?"

"That'll work."

"Be on time please."

"I got you."

She sucked her teeth. "Yeah, right." She hung up and immediately called Hook.

When Hook answered Brianna said, "Okay, nigga, I don't owe you nothing else. Your boy said he'll be here around six which means eight. So handle yours."

"Handle mines?" He asked sounding pissed off. "We straight as long as it's worth my while."

"Look, nigga, that ain't got shit to do with me. I called you and it's on so now we are even. *Ya heard?*"

Hook didn't say anything for a minute. "Bitch, it's over when I say it's over! *Ya heard?*"

Brianna sighed as she slammed down the phone. "How in the fuck did I ever got involved with a sorry-punk-ass nigga like that?" She said through clenched teeth.

Shadee didn't show up until a quarter after eight. When Brianna opened the door he grabbed her by her hair and gave her a big sloppy kiss. "What up B?" He asked while squeezing her ass.

"I'm on my way out. My girl is waiting on me. When it comes to me you never have a concept of the time do you?"

"Time is always on our side, B. And its time to break me off a little sumthin' sumthin'."

"I don't think so. If you would have come a little earlier, time would have been on your side. But I'm dressed, ready to go, and my girl is waiting on me."

"So B it's like that?"

"Right this minute? Yeah!" She tried to move his hands off her ass. "You always puttin' me on the back burner."

"Let me break you off then." He whispered into her ear. "You can spare a few minutes for that, can't you?"

Brianna really didn't have to think that one over because Shadee could give tha bomb head. It felt like he had two tongues and like he put his nose in it.

"That got your attention huh?" He laughed, sucked on her luscious lips some more, then picked her up and took her to the bedroom. "When are you gonna settle down for me?"

She slipped off her skirt as soon as he put her down. "When can you settle down for me?" She flipped it.

"Why you gotta always answer my question with a question?" He slapped her on the ass.

"Oowww! Why'd you do that?" She rolled her eyes at him.

"Answer my question." He watched her nipples stick out as he played with them.

"That feels good." She slid back onto the bed, spread her thighs and ran her feet across his chest. "Can I answer you later?" She moaned as he licked the inside of her thighs.

"Yeah, I guess you can do that." He said as he spread her swollen pussy lips, smiled at the sight of her clit sticking straight out and sucked one of his favorite juicy pussies until he couldn't suck anymore.

*   *   *

As Brianna washed up, Shadee began to pack six kilos of powder, and 8Gs in a bag. He took two of those and threw them on the coffee table for Brianna. "Yo, B!" he called. Brianna's apartment was one of the spots he used as a stash spot.

As Hook and his boy Rob sat in the car waiting for Shadee and watching his Benz, Shadee was kissing B on the lips. "Can I come by later?" he asked.

"Call me, okay?"

"Give me another kiss." He leaned over and kissed her then headed out the door.

"Here comes our boy." Rob, was anxious as hell as he grabbed his pipe and they sprang from the car. As Shadee went to unlock the car door, Rob smashed him over the head with the pipe causing Shadee to let out a loud grunt as he fell over. Hook grabbed the black duffel bag, then Rob stuffed Shadee's limp body onto the back seat. Hook started the car and as soon as he got it out of park, a forest green Hummer blocked him in and out jumped five of Shadee's boys.

Chapter 2

SHAN

"Who is it?"

"Who you expecting?"

A smile lit up Shan's face as she opened the door for her brother, Peanut, and his boy Nick who used to be Brianna's man. "I wasn't expecting you." She pushed up on her tippy toes and kissed him on the cheek. "So, to what do I owe the pleasure of this visit?"

"What you trying to say?" He asked as he walked in inspecting her apartment with Nick right behind him.

"Boy, don't even try it. I ain't trying to say nothing. I said it! Why you walking through my house like you a social worker or somebody?" She teased him as she was following behind him. "Have a seat, Nick."

Even though he wouldn't say it, he liked the gray and mauve color scheme she had going on throughout the entire apartment. But when you got to the bedroom it was full of black lacquer, red, yellow, light blue and purple. It was weird. It was as if you had stepped into another apartment.

"What? You tryna hide something or somebody?" He closed her bedroom door.

"Not from you." She pushed him into the living room onto the sofa. She plopped down beside him. Peanut had been her mother, father, brother and best friend since their parents were killed. Which caused them to have a very tight bond. "I don't know why you tryna front. Just say it. *Baby sis. I just love your beautiful apartment. It's better and cleaner than what all my hos got.*"

Peanut just smiled at her and Nick burst out laughing. "Oh, so you got jokes? It's not better than mines."

"Yeah, right. But guess what?"

"What?"

"I got the job and guess which one?" She was now off of the couch and hopping up and down.

"You making me dizzy. Sit your happy ass down."

"C'mon, Peanut. Guess which one?"

"I give up, Shan, so tell me."

"You ain't no fun no more. The prison job. I got the computer instructor job I was telling you about." Shan plopped back down next to Peanut once she saw the look on his face.

"You know I don't want you working at a men's prison. What if a riot or something breaks out? You the police, sis. You ain't gonna get no special treatment." Concern evident in his voice.

"Don't start." She jumped up again and headed out of the living room. "You know how much I wanted this one."

"Well, don't expect me to be happy for you. I don't feel right with my baby sister working around a bunch of crazy-ass niggas, Shan." He heard the bedroom door slam. "Shan! Shan!"

"What?" She snatched the door open.

"Fix me something to eat."

"Fix it yourself! I'm getting ready to shower and get dressed. Me and Brianna will be going out tonight to celebrate. At least she's happy for me."

"Yeah right! Brianna ain't never had no job, of course she's happy."

"Whatever!"

"What time y'all leaving and where are y'all going?"

Shan sucked her teeth. "I told her to be here at nine."

"Where y'all going?"

"You getting on my nerves now."

"Girl, you better tell me where you going," he warned as he stretched out on the sofa.

"I don't know where we're going. It's her treat."

"Well I suggest you find out."

"Nick, get your boy."

"Don't get me caught up in the middle of y'alls sibling rivalry."

"Oh, a'ight then. I see how you do. When B comes let her in. I gotta go and get ready."

"Shan, I'm serious, where y'all goin'?"

"I told you I didn't know. Ask her when she comes." Shan kept it moving and left Peanut and Nick sitting in the living room.

"Yo, what's up man? You know I don't need to be here when that bitch gets here. I'ma bust that thirsty bitch in her fuckin' mouth if I see her."

"Man, chill. I told you, you can't turn a ho into a housewife. I'ma kick it here for a while. Go pick that money up from Darnell and come back."

Nick raised his 6 foot, 4 inch frame up, gave Peanut a pound and headed for the door. "A' ight man. I'll swing back by."

"Later." Peanut kicked back and grabbed the remote. He knew that Nick's pride was hurt. Brianna got all she wanted to get outta his man and dumped him. Nick is still sprung over her.

* * *

Brianna came out of her building and went in the opposite direction, missing the activity behind her. She jumped into her champagne-colored Lexus and headed across town to Shan's.

Ten minutes later Brianna was knocking on the door.

"It's open." Peanut yelled.

Brianna stepped inside, smiled and licked her lips when she saw Peanut sitting on the couch. "Why is the door open?"

"Your boy Nick just left. You just missed him."

"Nigga please." She sat her Chanel bag down and stood directly in front of Peanut. "Where's your sister?"

"She's in there getting dressed."

Brianna got down on her knees and began kissing Peanut as she unzipped his pants.

"A'ight now. You gonna get us busted. Shan can come out the room any minute now and your man said he'll be right back." Peanut said as he slid his hand up her dress.

"So what are you saying?" She began slurping on the head of his dick.

"You playing wit fire, that's what I'm saying." He opened his legs wider and got in a better position. "Do you B, but make it quick." Peanut hit the mute button so that he could hear Shan, the slurping sounds B made on his dick and listen for Nick. "Damn . . . girl. Sssshit . . . "He grabbed the back of her head." "Whoaa, girl, why you stop?" His dick was hard as ten bricks and was sticking straight up.

"You got a condom?"

"C'mon, B." He grabbed her head. "What you need a condom for? You was almost done!"

"I want some dick, nigga."

"Girl, stop playing." His dick was throbbing so hard that he was ready to grab it and finish his self off.

She sucked her teeth, got up and pulled a condom outta her

Chanel bag. She ripped it open with her teeth and began putting it on a pissed-off Peanut.

"How you know I wanna fuck?" He watched her roll it down seductively on his dick with skill. "How 'bout I just want my dick sucked?"

Brianna turned around, pulled her dress up above her waist, bent over, holding on the coffee table and spread her legs. "Daddy, don't do me like this. C'mon, please."

Peanut stooped and rammed his dick in Brianna's hot, wet pussy. They both moaned out loud at the same time. Peanut thought his dick was gong to explode.

"Oh shit daddy! Give me that dick!"

"Keep it down, B." Peanut was ramming her so hard his balls were making slapping sounds. "Aaah, bitch!" He went to cumming and so did Brianna.

All you could hear was heavy breathing. Then Peanut's limp dick slid out and he pulled up his pants and fell back onto the couch. Just as Brianna stood up and pulled down her dress, Shan's bedroom door came open. Peanut hit the mute button on the TV and began flicking channels while Brianna made a bee-line for the bathroom.

"How long you been here?"

"A couple of minutes, girl, hold that thought." Brianna hurriedly closed the bathroom door.

"You still here?" Shan stuck her nose up at her brother. "What's that smell? You need to put your boots back on." She grabbed a can of air freshener and began spraying it throughout the rooms.

"Do you have to overdo it?"

Shan looked at her brother as if he was crazy. "I think you forgot whose house your in. It's time for you to go." *Knock, knock.* "Make yourself useful and get the door."

"It's your house, remember? You get the door." He teased. When she went to open it Peanut yelled, "It's open." And in stepped Nick.

Shan sucked her teeth and rolled her eyes at him.

"What I do?" Nick asked.

"Brought my brother over here."

"I didn't bring him, he brought me." "Nick casually said before turning to watch Brianna step out of the bathroom.

"You ready, girl?" She headed towards Shan's bedroom to avoid Nick. Shan followed behind her. "Close the door." She said with attitude. "What is he doing here?" Her arms were folded across her chest.

"I don't know. He came with Peanut." Shan shrugged it off. "How do I look?" She spun around in her tight leather all white Sean John shorts with the matching long sleeve jacket. "You like?"

"Girl, you look almost as good as me."

"Go 'head with that. Give props where props is due." Shan grabbed her leather Coach purse.

Brianna laughed. "A'ight, you got that. Those thigh high boots are bangin'! All you need now is a whip." She teased.

"Stop playin' and let's roll, I'm ready to get my party on."

"Me, too. If I can just get past the big, bad monster out there." B was referring to Nick.

"Girl, don't start with him. Let's just go." Shan turned off the bedroom light and led the way out. "Peanut, I'm out. Make sure you lock up."

Before Brianna could get to the door, Nick was up in her face. "Who the fuck you think I am?"

Brianna tried to walk around him but he grabbed her arm. "Peanut, get your boy." She tried to snatch it away.

"Nick," Peanut had jumped up off the couch. "C'mon man."

"Let me go, Nick. You're hurting me." Brianna warned

"C'mon man. Don't start this shit in my crib."

"Nut, let me holla at this bitch. Back up off of me man."

"Take this shit outside." Peanut was trying to free Brianna's arm from Nick's grip.

"We ain't taking nothing outside. I don't have shit to say to the nigga, so why is he harassing me?" When she snatched away from him he hauled off to punch her in the face but Peanut blocked the blow and pushed him towards the front door. Shan opened it up and grabbed his arm.

"Nick, I know you ain't swing at her in my house!" She was pulling him out into the hallway.

"I'm not even gonna let that nigga get me excited and ruin my evening. Punk!" Brianna yelled at him as the front door closed.

"You ain't right, B! You know that, don't you? I want you to chill out!" Peanut told her.

"I'm chilled; you need to be tellin' your boy that."

"I'ma get with him. Where are y'all going tonight?"

"That new club out on the Eastside called The Spot, you coming through? When am I going to see you again?" Brianna was like, *later for Nick I'm tryna get with you again.*

"You can see me right now." Peanut leaned over and gave her a kiss.

"Stop playing, Peanut, I'm serious."

"I'm serious, too. I can hit it right quick."

"You gonna get us busted."

"You wasn't saying that earlier."

"C'mon, Brianna." Shan burst in the door. "He's in the car." She looked from her brother to Brianna. "You okay?"

"I'm fine."

"What time you coming home?" Peanut asked Shan.

"I'm grown. I'll be here when I get here. Now come on B. Lock the door, Peanut."

They drove in silence as the Lex pumped the music of Ashanti, Vivian Greene and Heather Hadley.

"Yo, you know you did Nick wrong, right?"

"Girl, fuck these niggas! I'll be glad when you wake the fuck up."

"I'm just saying B, you reap what you sow. That nigga held you down the whole time you was on lock. Then when he got knocked, you ain't give the nigga that same love back. But when he got out and came back up, you got back in . . ."

"Until I got tired of him and it was a wrap." Brianna cut Shan off and finished off her sentence. "So what? Shit, he'll get over it." I'm sure this ain't the first time he got used for the trick that he is."

"I don't know what to say about you."

"Whatever, ho. Now tell me about this Calvin."

"Hold up, guess who had the audacity to call me last night?"

"Who? And don't think I'm letting you get away with not telling me about Calvin."

"Girl, shut up and guess who had the nerve to call?"

"Derrick."

"Nope."

"Jay."

"Nope."

"Girl, who?"

"Kris."

"Aw hell, naw! Did you talk to him or hang up on his ass? I hope you called the police and told them. Ain't that violating his restraining order? You should have let Peanut kill his ass when he wanted to. I hate the way he would bruise you up. You didn't talk to him, did you?"

"No. I hung up. Shit I should have killed him myself. Police officer or not."

"Hell yeah. What did he say?"

"I hung up. I didn't even want to hear it."

"That's what I'm talkin' bout." Brianna high-fived Shan. "Fuck him! I wanna hear about Calvin. Why is he such a big secret? Is he that fine? Don't worry, you're my girl, I won't take him from you!"

If Shan only knew. Brianna's grimy ass fucked her ex Kris on several occasions resulting in a pregnancy that she aborted.

"Bitch, pleeze! He is very fine but he is not your type. Meaning, he's not a baller or a trick. He's a businessman."

"What kind of business?"

"I met him when I went to get my brakes fixed. He owns an auto repair shop on the Southside."

"I hear you. So why haven't I met him?"

"Girl, please, I haven't heard back from him."

"What do you mean? Why not."

"That's a whole 'nother story?

"What happened? What happened, ho?" Brianna prodded.

"I don't want to talk about him."

"C'mon, Shan. Tell me." The suspense was now more than she could stand.

Getting agitated, Shan spat out, "We fucked and I haven't heard from him since! Okay?"

"What? No shit? That ain't your style, Shan. How'd you let him play you like that? Please tell me you got a couple of grand outta the nigga! I know I taught you better than that!" Brianna said with much attitude.

"Girl, please. You the last person I'll let teach me anything."

"So what happened? Did you or didn't you get some paper?"

"No, I wasn't tryna hustle the nigga for no dollars but we'd been vibin' off one another, and he made plans to take me to Las Vegas the weekend of my birthday. I told you that."

"Damn, that reminds me. We haven't kicked it since your birthday?"

"No, we haven't. You've been doing what you do best, hoing around, hustlin' niggas, and I've been doing what I do, working and job hunting."

"I'ma act like you didn't say that. But for the record, don't hate the player, hate the game. Now, finish telling me about Las Vegas. And please tell me you at least milked Las Vegas until it couldn't be milked anymore."

"Brianna, do you ever rest from getting your hustle on?"

"No, I don't."